SOMETHING INFINITE

Something Infinite

Eddie S. Pierce

Copyright © 2011 by Eddie S. Pierce.

Library of Congress Control Number: 2011914758
ISBN: Hardcover 978-1-4653-5292-7
　　　Softcover 979-8-6015-6758-9
　　　Ebook 978-1-4653-5293-4

All rights reserved. No part of this book may be reproduced or transmitted in any form or by any means, electronic or mechanical, including photocopying, recording, or by any information storage and retrieval system, without permission in writing from the copyright owner.

This is a work of fiction. Names, characters, places and incidents either are the product of the author's imagination or are used fictitiously, and any resemblance to any actual persons, living or dead, events, or locales is entirely coincidental.

This book was printed in the United States of America.

Contents

Abstract..9
Foreword..11

Saturday

The Phone Call..15

Thursday

Seron 2.0...21
Chi-Town..26
Back Down Memory Lane..31
Black Satin...35
Seron 1.0...42

Friday

Calvin...49
Regina...54
A Dreadlocked Mystery..58
Where My Girls At...61
M & M..66
My First Time with a Barber..70

Saturday

Commitment . . . YIKES!...79
Abomination...83
Serious Conversations..87
Status Update...91

Sunday

A Bit More Slack 101
Past Meets Present 105
Epitome 109
Dreams Do Come True 111

Monday

Resolution 121
Excerpt for Love: From Behind 125
Something Infinite Discussion Questions 127
"Praise for Love: Something Infinite" 131
Author Biography: 133

To my God, my family, my friends and everyone else who helped me to live this story. Thank you for your loving support, encouragement and your feedback.

Special Thanks:

Photographer/Creative Director: Stephen Evans (Stephen Evans Photography)
Assistant Creative Director: Michael Tilley
Makeup Artist: Julie Duncan
Model: Kenneth (Kenny J) Jackson (as Seron)
Model: Brian Ricardo Sims (as Rodney)
Model: Louis E. Green (as Calvin)
Photographer: Horace Hardy (H2 Productions)
Graphic Artist: Whitney Napoleon (Napoleon Design)
Remimakuo Media Club
Iya Barake: Gloss Magazine Online
Gregg Shapiro: WisconsinGazette.com
LaToya Cross: N'Digo Magazine Online
James Earl Hardy
Bon Manger Catering LLC
Scott Free: Homolatte
QuickClick Media
DJ Scott "GucciRoxx" Rivers: The High Society
K Dock Media
PWEconcepts LLC
Chicago Black Gay Men's Caucus
Chicago LGBTQ Professionals
Sweetthangs Bakery
Follicle Hair Salon
Southside Help Center
Clairalice Campini, Ph.D.
Dennis Ray Knight Jr.
Pastor Shirley Pollion-Hines
Ray Silkman: Silkscreen Production

ABSTRACT

Love: Something Infinite is a work of fiction which borrows situations and scenery from my experiences and aspirations. The characters are parodies, composites and/or archetypes inspired by real life counterparts. Following after the tradition of works by bestselling authors such as James Baldwin, E Lynn Harris and James Earl Hardy this novel attempts to effectively illustrate lesser explored expressions of romantic love, loss, and self acceptance. In addition several original works of poetry have been inserted intermediately; adding further emotional emphasis to several key points of the narrative. Finally and perhaps most importantly, this novel adds to the voices of the HIV/AIDs infected and affected for the purposes of further informing the public about the emotional implications involved in this epidemic and dispelling the common misconception that such a diagnosis is a "death sentence."

Sincerely,
Eddie S. Pierce

FOREWORD

Eddie S. Pierce, Jr. captures the very essence of society amongst African-American homosexual males **during this age and time**. Not only are we given taken on a journey through reading, but we are able to enter the life and mind of the main character, Seron, as he traverses through life and all of its obstacles. The life, thoughts, and emotions of Seron can be an example for anyone living today who feels as though they are an outcast looking for acceptance for being who they truly are. Never has a work of literature resonated for me, as a reader, more than this novel. We have witnessed throughout history literature being a vital part of any movement and this novel proves to be in the forefront of understanding the Gay Rights and Equal Rights movements. As we embark on the brink of new dimensions, *Love: Something Infinite* will be among those literary works of art that will be looked upon and studied as an integral part of history.

Dennis Ray Knight, Jr.

SATURDAY

THE PHONE CALL

Waking up more exhausted than I was when I passed out, I motion to rise only to find myself still encircled by his arms.

"Where you going, baby boi?"

"Rodney, baby," I begin to sigh, but instead of getting up, I somewhat reluctantly surrender to the sensation of his warm breath against my back, the plea from his deep voice, and the memory of the intimacy that brought on the 2nd involuntary midmorning nap.

Mentally I thank God for the cool central air which quietly labors against the brutal August Las Vegas heat just outside of my apartment. Rodney, somewhat clumsy, switches our sweet spoon into a missionary position. The high I feel from the weight of him on top of me allies itself with the intoxication of his full lips and tongue courting mine. Our smooth bodies slowly slide against each other, rekindling the flame while his fingers scout my terrain. A sudden awareness breaks through.

Those aren't scouts; they're ten treacherous decoys!

Before I can protest, the enemy is at the gate; my defenses evaporate into the ether and my fortress is invaded, again.

An eternity and an infinite number of kisses later, we fall back into a debilitating exhaustion.

"How do we ever leave the bed on a Saturday morning?" I ask.

I quickly learn that my dialogue is a monologue as I hear Rodney breathing deeply. As I contemplate indulging in a third nap, a long and loud beep from my cell phone demands my return to the conscious world. For a split second, I'm surprised that I didn't hear the sound of Gwen Stefani's aspirations to rise to the status of a rich girl blaring from my new favorite tin toy. As I reach for the phone, Rodney's arms lay claim to my waist once again, and consciousness answers the door to common sense. I doubt I would have heard a plane crash between Rodney snoring and all this morning sex. Out of habit, I look at the caller ID before checking the voice mail. Three calls from my least favorite person—the household of Unknown Caller. Now curiosity and irritation sit down to take a morning coffee with consciousness and common sense. Determined to uncover the identity of the vile imps that have intruded upon some much-needed rest, I dial 1, accessing my voice mail.

"You have three messages. Message 1, 8:31 a.m. Marked Urgent."

Nothing, I think as the cell phone replays a completely silent recording.

I press 7 with a bit more force than necessary, deleting the blank message.

"Message 2, 9:35 a.m. Marked Urgent."

"Seron, I know you don't know me, but my name is Sean. I am a close friend of Calvin's."

Another fool is born. God bless him, I think to myself.

"I found your number in his cell phone," the message continues.

And you are calling me because . . . , I wonder, twirling my finger in the air, giving Sean the signal to wrap it up.

"Please call me back on Calvin's phone as soon as you get this message."

"Message 3, 11:53 a.m. Marked Urgent."

"Seron, it's Sean again. I really didn't want to tell you this over the phone, let alone in the form of a voice mail, but Calvin is in the hospital, and he's really not doing so well. He would never forgive me if I didn't at least get word to all his closest friends just in case . . . well . . . Look, I know there is a lot of time and distance between you two, but he really needs to see you, and I think that you need to see him. Please just call me back."

* * *

"Calvin, we really need to talk. It's been three months."

"I can't right now," he said, still refusing to look my way.

I looked at him, trying in vain to will him to face me, but he wouldn't.

"Okay," I sighed. "I'm going to leave, then."

I stood and turned to go. I heard the remote fall to the couch. He quickly, desperately grabbed my arm. I heard his ragged breathing before I looked back down to him. Calvin looked at me, his eyes pleading for understanding, for forgiveness.

"I just . . . can't do this anymore."

I was surprised to hear his voice crack over the sound of my own heart breaking. The sensation of infinity that we had always shared finally collapsed as our hands let go. I turned away for what I believed to be forever that day and closed the door behind me.

Eboni's Loss

Apprehensive anxious meetings
Expectations fulfilled
Sweetness given form
Southern Comfort personified
Mahogany guised intelligence

Discovering poetic inspirations
Achieving something new
Minds finding common ground
Embraces expressing sincerity
Instant synchronous affection
Interlocking bodies at rest
Mutual hidden desires
Pointless confining reservations
Voiceless forsaken feelings
Advances not attempted
An amorous affair incomplete

3/7/02

Seron Wright Jr.

THURSDAY

Seron 2.0

There it is again, that malicious mingled feeling of failure, dread, and despair that comes over me every time I return home—be it by land, sea, and, in this case, American Airlines. I usually overcome the failure with the quickest ease. After all, it isn't as if I'm returning to my mama's house—the graduate, the pride of the family and yet shamefully unemployed. It took four and a half years of undergraduate study at Northeastern Missouri State University, five years of employment and graduate study at the University of Nevada-Las Vegas, but my first novel *Light and Darkness*, was finally deemed worthy of Tor Publishing. My reward—a fifty-thousand-dollar advance and a contract for two more novels within the next two and a half years, each paying their own advance. Probably not the greatest deal in the history of publishing, but still good considering the economy. Now I can proclaim myself a published, paid novelist. This isn't something I have to do often, thanks to my director of public relations, known to me as Mom. Dread and despair—well, those are two entirely different beasts of a more sinister order.

"Does your luggage have a lock, sir?" asks a rather attractive slightly older pecan-tanned gentleman working the baggage-scanning station at McCarran International Airport.

"No, it doesn't," I reply.

As I move to lift my bags onto the conveyor belt, his large hand intercepts me.

"Let me help you with that," he says with a warm smile, framed by a thin neat goatee that is just starting to gray.

"Thank you," I answer while admiring his muscular arms at work, the biceps just visible, thanks to his navy blue short-sleeved uniform shirt.

He turns slightly to put my bags through the scanner, and I catch a glimpse of a well-shaped butt as well.

"My pleasure," he responds, returning to his full erect height of 6'3". "Enjoy your trip."

He extends that powerful hand to me. We shake hands.

In the next hour, I work my way to the gate and board the plane with my carry-on bag and a bit of anticipation. Before the demons of my past can fully take hold, I reach for salvation in the form of my iPod. While I take out my laptop, preparing to do some outlining of my second novel, I notice that the flight is fairly empty.

"Is anyone sitting here?" asks a familiar voice, calling my attention from the window.

I look up to see the baggage handler from earlier pointing to the aisle seat beside me, in which I had left my carry-on bag and a sports jacket.

"Um, no," I answer despite my confusion.

"Do you mind?"

"No."

He takes my things and carefully places them in the overhead compartment with his camera bag, giving me an impressive view of his flat stomach and a solid chest trying to escape a simple button-down royal blue shirt. Then he situates his strapping frame into the seat beside me, puts on some headphones, and relaxes. The plane taxis and takes off.

"You are now cleared to use any approved electronic devices," calls the head flight attendant over the intercom as the plane finally levels off in midair.

I start up my laptop and pull up the Word document containing my latest manuscript.

"What are you working on?" asks my new neighbor. "If you don't mind my asking."

"A novel," I answer, looking up from the screen at him. "I hope."

"You are a writer? Cool," he says. "Matthew," he says, extending his hand again.

"Seron," I reply, shaking his hand again. "Excuse me, Matthew, but haven't we met already?"

"You can call me Matt. Yeah, I figured you'd remember me."

"So are you following me?"

"Would that be a bad thing?" Matt answers with another smile.

I can feel the mixture of nervousness and annoyance radiating from my face.

He laughs.

"Well?" I ask again very deliberately.

"I'm sorry," he apologizes, with one defensive hand in the air. "I didn't mean to make you uncomfortable. To be honest, I was planning on using the free flight privileges I get as an employee to go to Chicago this weekend. When I saw the open seat next to you, I decided to sit here."

"Why?" I ask, fishing for answers I'm already sure I possess.

"Do you really have to ask?"

Matt takes full advantage of the armrest and leans in closer. He smells nice, fresh. A hint of soap and Nautica Sport. He obviously showered and changed out of his uniform back at the airport.

"I don't like to make assumptions."

"Neither do I, but I believe in following my instincts."

I smile to myself.

"So are you involved?"

His eyes dance in my direction.

I guess I didn't affix my straight-boy face this morning. Even though my level of self-acceptance has grown these past ten years, I'm still not altogether comfortable with someone guessing that I'm gay. It is, however, always a pleasant surprise when the "someone" is someone I'm at least moderately interested in, but it still surprises me when a guy approaches me.

"Yes, I am involved."

But if I wasn't . . . Wow!

"Well," he says with a little less enthusiasm in his eyes, "is he treating you right?"

"Yeah, he is doing pretty good."

"Good to hear. So . . . you interested in making friends?"

"Uh . . ."

"By friends I only mean *friends*."

"That's cool," I reply, my body relaxing.

"Would you like something to drink?" asks one of the flight attendants in the aisle.

"I'll have a Jack Daniels," Matt answers. "You want something?" he asks, turning to me. "It's on me."

"Vodka and cranberry, please."

I close my laptop as the drinks are prepared and handed to us.

"So, my new friend Matt, what do you do aside from the obvious?"

"Working at the airport is my job," he begins. "I'm a freelance photographer."

"Now that is cool. So you fly for free to the places that you are going to shoot."

"Shhh," he gestures, putting his finger to his lips. "That's my secret mission."

He flashes that full-on-Kodak smile again.

"Ah, so you're a triple threat," I say behind my plastic cup.

"I hope that is a compliment."

"I was referring to your having brains as well as brawn and beauty."

"A perfect catch for a cute, creative writer. Maybe one day I'll find an available one."

I don't need a mirror to see that my face most likely matches the cranberry in my cup. Our friendly, flirtatious chat makes the three-hour flight from Vegas to Chicago fly by both literally and figuratively.

"Maybe we can talk about collaborating over drinks sometime back in Vegas," says Matt, giving me his card as we gather our bags in the baggage claim at O'Hare International Airport. "I could do some cover art for your novels."

"Sounds like a good idea," I reply as we exchange a friendly hug and part ways.

Walking to the rental car lot, I take a look at the card. It is a simple photograph of a beach at sunset.

Iris Photography
Matthew Davis
702-785-4092
www.irisphotography.com

And on the back:
Let me know if your "situation" changes.
Matt 702-665-4459
P.S. Can't blame me for trying.

I smile to myself. Turning around, I see that Matt has been watching me walk away. He nods and smiles. I wave and continue on my way.

CHI-TOWN

Rather than drive directly home, I speed past the I-90 Harlem exit, heading east. Now memory takes the driver's seat as I recall all the nocturnal journeys along this same, much-worn, very beaten path. The rainbow-colored neon lights on the strip of north Halsted, which marked the beginning and end of Boys' Town, are as bright in my mind's eye as the sunlight of the present day. Being the only gay person I knew, closeted or otherwise, I spent the better part of my final college vacation in various clubs, bars, and sex shops in search of something, anything I could identify with. The well-known north-side haven for gays and lesbians primarily catered to brothers and sisters of a *lighter hue*, with just a few of us brown folks sprinkled in for seasoning. The latter were more like the former than me, so my search met with mixed results.

"What does the *Prop House* even look like in daylight?" I wonder while making the left at the BP Amoco on Elston in search of one of my old nightspots in the Chicago Warehouse District.

It wasn't until I had finally graduated undergrad that I began to frequent the Prop House and a number of other somewhat hidden refuges tailor-made for those of us whose culture went deeper than the melanin in our skin. Even they only temporarily satisfied me. Unfortunately, I have to lump my romance with Calvin in that finite category too.

"Well, I've stalled as much as possible," I sigh, sitting parked in front of the club. "Calvin and the hospital can wait, but I have to go *home* at some point."

Executing one of those bold U-turns that Chicago drivers are known the world over for, I head back to the expressway and make my way home. As I turn on to the block, I notice that time seems to have stood still in the old neighborhood, which marked the end of the city limits and the beginning of the suburbs of Oak Park and Elmwood. The summer sun attempts to penetrate the thick foliage of the oak trees lining the street. While stepping out of my rental, I make the last-minute adjustments to my blazer and my attitude. I remind myself that I'm going home, not reporting to the County.

"Damn it, why can't I ever remember to bring my key when I come home?"

After a necessarily forceful knock and a few seconds, he comes to the door standing every bit of 6'1" and damn near a solid two hundred pounds—my father, Jeremy Washington, well, my stepfather. Despite the distant everyday presence of my biological father in my life, this man has planted figurative seeds in my life just as important as the literal one that got me here.

"What, you lost your key?" he asks.

It wouldn't be a trip home if he didn't ask.

"Naw, I just forgot it as usual."

A quick but mutually sincere, manly hug finds my face in the familiar middle of his chest. After all these years and everything that came with them, I still have to wonder how is it that I not only turned out to be gay but also moderately effeminate, with two fathers like this consistently in my life. Well, I'm sure I'm not the only one who questions that. Rather than let those demons have me this early into the visit, I cast the thought down.

"You looking good, man. I guess things are alright out there in the desert."

"Yeah, it's cool. Not home, of course, but you know I never cared for Chicago winter."

We walk the five steps down into the basement den that he has perfected even more since I left five years ago. He takes his place in the recliner and I on the love seat. With that, my first unscheduled but much-anticipated interview is under way.

"So I see you finally decided to spring for the Comcast digital cable, huh?" I ask, looking around with wide-eyed admiration.

"Yeah, man, that satellite was just too much money and too much trouble," he replied, recovering the remote.

"I'm sure that DV-R option is what won Mom over."

"Yeah. She should be here any minute. She was supposed to leave early, but you know she can't ever seem to leave out from that job."

We both kind of laugh that off. The conversation is pretty much about nothing, seeing as how we keep in touch over the big things, plus I think it occurs to him that I would really hate to repeat everything all over when my mom comes in. He throws me for a somewhat expected, or should I say dreaded, twist when he does ask, "So you find a church out there yet?"

"Not yet," I answer, trying not to visibly squirm. "Aside from doing my private devotions every morning, I've still been visiting a few places. My boss goes to one of them."

Well, that's what I said, but the truth is, I spend more Sunday mornings in bed with Rodney or making him breakfast, just to get back into bed. Two facts that I'm not altogether comfortable with, but that's nothing compared to the level of discomfort those truths would give the majority of my family and friends.

"Okay. I know you still send your tithes back this way. That's good, but you know you need to find one. Don't get out there and forget about the Lord."

Thankfully, before that conversation can go any further, I hear the sound of keys in the door.

"Where is he?" my mom, Esther, practically sings, rushing into the house.

Funny, she's usually running directly into the bathroom. Love is truly a powerful thing when it overrides the bladder.

"There's my firstborn son."

We hug.

Why do I have to move so far away to appreciate this? I wonder.

"Let me run to the bathroom."

Just then, it hits me that the rest of the house is more quiet than usual.

"I forgot, Eric moved out," I say, turning back to my father. "I know you all checked out his place."

"Man," he sighs, visibly exercising restraint. "It's . . . well, it's not that studio you had, but like I told you back then, he could have got something better for his money, but that's what he wanted to do."

"Yeah, I remember."

I recall our discussion and my first place. It was a fairly large studio in Chicago's affluent yet over-priced Hyde Park neighborhood, far from luxurious. It had five windows, all staring into the wall of the building only six feet away from mine. The Metra and freight trains directly behind the building sent a slight but regularly scheduled tremble throughout the apartment. The sounds of the couple wrestling from above, the bachelor's blaring music below, and the drug dealer's transactions across the hall constantly pressed up against the paper door, floor, and ceiling. There was always something going on.

"It's okay, though, right? I mean it's up to code," I laugh, continuing our discussion about my brother, Eric. "He didn't tell me much about it or anything else over the phone or in e-mail."

"Yeah, yeah, all of that is cool. He said he'll be over this weekend for dinner," he replies while aimlessly channel-surfing.

"And where is Regina? I thought she didn't have classes past three o'clock on Thursday."

"Well, you know we got your sister that car and she just be gone. But not like you used to be for days at a time."

Ouch!

That last low blow is loaded with more memories of my earlier adventures. Exploring my *alternative* orientation under the cover of darkness. All the nights in the dives that passed for clubs and bars. Countless bad blind dates with the rare refreshing experience of meeting someone who didn't just share my supposed sexual *preference* but was also, at the least, interesting to talk to. *Alternative? Preference?* When was I ever presented with the opportunity to select the *conventional* versus *alternative* as my *preference*? Maybe it's the writer in me, but that seems like a fucked-up word choice. At any rate, it was a very dangerous time now that I think back on all the things that could have happened to me. Perhaps, the reality of what happened between Calvin and me keeps the cosmic scales balanced. A momentary sensation that could have, should have lasted forever.

"But she also runs around with those girlfriends of hers that stay on that UIC campus," he continues, oblivious to my quick trek back in time.

"That lil'lil' girl thinks she's slick," says Mom, coming back down to sit on the other end of the love seat closest to Dad.

I'm still sitting by the door ready to bolt. Even now, we have our assigned positions, he and I at opposite extremes and she in the dual role of a mediator and being a "cohesive."

"There's got to be a boy," she half-laughs.

"What!" I exclaim. "When I last talked with her, Sunday I think it was, she was still talking about . . . What was his name? Jonathan."

"Hmm, she says they're just friends, but . . ."

Suddenly, I notice that Dad is being very quiet.

"Well, I've got my eye on her," Mom continues, changing the subject.

I guess she noticed Dad's silence too.

"So I'm sure you two have talked about some of everything. What did I miss?"

"Nothing you and I don't discuss every day courtesy of your job's toll-free line," I answer.

Which still isn't much, despite the daily hour-long conversations. There is a whole life of love, occasional indulgence in unspeakable substances, and a host of other subjects not suitable for a mother's ears.

"I'm surprised Sprint hasn't sent you their phone bill," I laugh, meticulously steering this conversation through some very choppy, rock-filled waters.

For the record, they think that this is just a spur-of-the-moment, I'm-so-homesick visit. Well, it is partially true. I haven't been back to Chicago for a little over a year, even missing the major holidays.

"After all these years working for that company, I should send them mine," she snaps back. "So you let your dad know you made it?"

"I'm actually going to call him when we finish talking and then run down the list calling all the family and friends. How is Grandma Barnes?"

"She is doing okay," my stepfather answers. "She'll be here for Sunday dinner."

The conversational minutia goes on for about another hour, the three of us diplomatically avoiding troublesome topics, namely, my lifestyle and current same-sex relationship of which they are aware but don't condone. My idea that all this physical distance and discreet chitchat preserve my family relationship is reaffirmed.

BACK DOWN MEMORY LANE

Finally, I make it to my old room, which has been remodeled into a semiregular guest room for Grandma Barnes. Despite the painted walls, new bed, and coordinated bedding, the familiar sensation of claustrophobia attempts to surface. It is crazy that I found so much comfort in this tiny fortress of solitude while feeling trapped within it at the same time.

Hmm . . . Is tan paint an effective gag for these walls?

Nearly ten years of pain, confusion, tears, loneliness, fantasies, and nocturnal and midday emissions all occasionally punctuated by slivers of contentment and joy. A suffocating identity slowly breaking through an icy surface, grasping for air.

"Damn it. I've only been here for, what, three hours and I'm already tripping," I mumble to myself.

For the second time today, I fight the urge to go in, to give in to emotion. Instead, I situate my bags. While I unpack, I notice an old three-ring binder.

"Mom keeps everything."

I pause to reacquaint myself with the crude short stories and a few poems written throughout my childhood and my youth.

A montage of memory explodes in my head. The long summer vacations I spent at Grandma's house with my brother, cousins, and youngest uncle and aunt rushed forward. The joys of uncomplicated childhood rejuvenate my young adult reality. Long, hot days in the park. Wet afternoons writing. Humid evenings tearing through Grandma's house. Late cool nights of Spades and Monopoly. My heart struggles against the confines of rocky romances, paying bills—one unfulfilling job after another. The trappings of adult responsibility. As I tuck the notebook in one of my bags, I long for the ability to chase nostalgia down the rabbit hole in search of infinitely more simple times coupled with nearly abandoned, artistic ambitions.

I finish unpacking and begin making my calls. Dad doesn't answer at home or his cell.

"Why does he even have a cell phone?"

And the voice mail still isn't set up.

I make two relatively quick but meaningful phone calls to both grandmothers. Confirmations of safe travel, love, and dinner this coming Sunday.

While wrapping things up with Grandma Earlean, call-waiting kicks in.

"Okay, Grandma, I'll try to come up and see you while visiting Dad."

I switch over.

"Wassup, playboy?"

"Nothing much, man, just trying to get in touch with a celebrity," chuckles Rodney, sending a smile through the phone matching my own. "You might know him. He's a world-renowned author. Goes by the name Seron Wright Jr."

"Celebrity, huh?" looking myself over in the full-length mirror that covers the closet door.

"Well, you know, you jet set off at the drop of a hat. You, no doubt, over there getting the celebrity treatment."

"Yeah. They're planning a dinner."

"And you too busy with all yo fans to remember the president of yo fan club."

"Baby, I'm sorry," I sigh into the phone.

That is something I'll never get right—notifying all interested parties when I touch down.

"Don't sweat it, I know you with yo peoples. Besides, I wanted to hear from you, so I called and now I'm hearing from you."

"I promise I'm glad you called."

"So you miss me?"

"Nope," I smile to myself.

"Oh hell naw," he laughs. "You know you gonna pay for that one the next time I got yo ass pinned to this bed."

"How you know I ain't trying to hype you up to punish me later?"

"Dat's wussup! You know I can be there in three hours and make that happen. I ain't been to the Chi since I was a shawty."

"Come on now, you know the deal."

I almost miss the moment my reflected smile inverts.

"You know I'm fuckin' with you, baby. I know the boundaries, and I told you I ain't trying to cross them, for now. I still don't see why we couldn't just get a room."

"Rodney," I sigh, "I already told you—"

"Yeah, yeah. 'You gonna be running around all weekend and it ain't fair to me to be dragged along.' Come on, man. I had my tongue in yo ass just this morning. You don't think I deserve the truth, or am I just some piece of trade now?"

"Rodney," I say his name and my breath barely getting around gritted teeth.

"Well, that is the way you treating me."

"Look, okay, okay. We've talked about stuff like this before."

I mentally strategize how to bring this conversation to a subtle but abrupt end.

"Refresh my memory, then."

"Look, I hate walking up and down the street and people already think I'm gay, you by my side, then it becomes 'I wonder if they fucking. The little one is obviously gay.'"

The suspicions would definitely **begin** with me. Rodney is that hot, somewhat hypermasculine, 6'2", 185 lb., bald, goatee-wearing, baritone-voiced, alley-basketball-playing, chocolate-double-dipped Adonis. People would sooner believe that Tupac (God rest his soul) was on the Green Line EL promoting his new double-disc album, featuring the Notorious B.I.G. (God rest *his* soul) on tracks 1-15 than think that Rodney was gay. But he still adds supporting evidence to anyone's assumption that I am gay. When the two of us are in public, he unconsciously tends to loom over me like my own Secret Service. That is when there isn't the appearance of any competition for my attention. In the latter case, his normally friendly demeanor develops a *green*-tinged edge. The most suspicious might guess that in an alternate reality, he could be bisexual, but not gay.

"I figured it was something like that," he replies somewhat smugly.

"Well, since you know so damn much, why you asking so many damn questions?"

"'Cus you needed to say it. Dammit, baby. You got to get over that shit. I mean you told damn near yo whole family and all yo closest friends, right?"

"Yeah," I sigh.

"And all the people who matter still got love for you, right?"

"Yeah."

"And you got the privilege of Mr. Black Satin as yo man."

I laugh.

"Oh, so you gonna laugh in a man's face when he speaking truth and trying to make yo ass feel good? I should hang up this phone."

"No, baby, no. Don't hang up. I'm sorry," I struggle to regain my composure. "I was just remembering the first time you called yourself Mr. Black Satin."

"Aaww shit, Hamburger Mary's!" he hollers through the phone.

"You walked into that club in them leather pants and cowboy boots." My giggles threatening to return.

"Nigga don't trip. That's how I did my thing in Dallas. Had niggas and chicks trippin'. And I remember you saying 'cowboys are the sexiest thing walking on three legs.'"

"Oh, so now you trying to quote me. Nigga, I'm the writer. And for the record, I told you that you shouldn't wear those too many places aside from the stage or my bedroom."

"Hmmm, okay, Mr. Writer. At least you starting to sound more like the man I'm feeling and not some crying faggot."

I'm thankful we aren't having this conversation in person; otherwise, he'd see my eyes roll. Then I'd be in trouble all over again.

"Yeah, you are good for setting me off one minute and then cooling me down the next."

The call-waiting beeps.

"Damn, baby, that's my dad."

"Cool, cool. Just call *yo* daddy if you need me. And I better hear from you tonight."

"You got it, sexy daddy."

BLACK SATIN

"Hamburger Mary's!"
It was the oddest name for a club that I could imagine.
"Don't let the name fool you," said Lee. "It is really a hot spot."

It had been three months since I moved from Chicago to Las Vegas to work and study at UNLV, and I hadn't checked out the nightlife yet. So when my coworker Lee suggested it, I gave in. Well, to be honest, it took everything in me not to jump out of my skin with excitement. I had been hiding the crush that I had on him from the first day we met during the interview process. It took all my resolve to get through that interview without getting lost in those dark brown eyes, not to be mesmerized by his gorgeous light-bronze face. The last couple of months working so close to his compact swimmer's build within the campus Academic Advising office were the sweetest torture.

On the one hand, I was seeking hints as to his sexuality while attempting to conceal my own. While he wasn't hypermasculine and didn't make the usual boasts of sexual conquest with every woman since Eve, I was so sure that we weren't playing in the same league. In the end, I decided that the pain of a hidden attraction was a lesser evil than ruining the only potentially good friendship I had this far from home. But now he was asking me to hang out with him, alone.

* * *

"So what do you think?" Lee asked as I set up my shot at one of the club's four pool tables.

I aimed and took my shot. Number 2 ball, the side pocket. A long-range shot. My weakness. I missed.

"Yeah, this place is pretty cool," I replied, standing up to take in the rest of the club. I wondered if there were any decent gay clubs, though.

The crowd on the fairly large dance floor grooved to a mix of hip-hop, rap, R&B, and surprisingly, reggae. I watched, hopefully not too longingly as Lee bent over our table, across from me and prepared to take his shot. Against my better judgment, I watched him extend his toned forearms, flex well-defined biceps and a muscular back that showed through his Calvin Klein white silk tee. The only thing that could have topped that scene would have been to see it from behind. From there, I could have also stolen a glimpse of his high, round butt. My daily dose of eye candy. A tingling in my own CKs warned me that I had looked too long. Out of desperation, I looked to the dance floor and spotted something not quite as interesting.

"What's wrong?" he asked as he noticed my line of sight, in between clearing the table.

"Is there a stage in the middle of the dance floor?"

"Oh yeah. They sometimes have talent shows," he explained while I watched the eight ball and all hope of me catching up to him sink into the right-corner pocket. "You know, open mic nights, musicians, and all that," Lee continued as he stood up, grabbed his beer, and took a drink.

As if on cue, the music stopped and the lights came up a bit.

"Ladies and gentlemen," called the DJ from a hidden booth. "Please welcome back Mr. Black Satin himself, Rodney!"

There was a thunderous applause throughout the club as the bodies on the dance floor parted like the Red Sea forming a path right before me. Seemingly for me. My breath was stolen with surprise. I began to raise my hands, my mind already saying there must be some mistake. Just then, I felt a large hand gently squeeze my right shoulder.

"Excuse me," said a deep baritone over my left shoulder.

The hand swept across my shoulder blades and down to rest in the small of my back. I turned and saw him, wearing the most wondrous ebony complexion and an ivory smile.

"I'm sorry," I replied, obviously startled.

"No problem, playboy," he said with a wink.

As he walked past, I finally noticed that he was carrying a saxophone. He made his way to the floor with the sexiest swagger that demanded my full attention. Out of pure habit, I looked down from his sky blue muscle-filled T-shirt, beyond the form-fitting jet-black leather pants and saw shiny black cowboy boots. He took the stage with a well-earned confidence. Without further ado, he positioned the sax in front of him and applied the juiciest but moderately full lips around the mouthpiece and began to play Jill Scott's "He Loves Me." As the smooth silky sound filled the air, I allowed myself to imagine the two hands that fingered the sax caressing the nape of my neck and massaging the small of my back. His sweet lips pressed against mine.

"He's pretty good, huh?" Lee asked as he stood beside me.

"Uh, yeah," I replied, obviously startled.

"He comes through our office from time to time. Rodney's an undergrad at UNLV by day, studying physical therapy, but this"—he nodded Rodney's way with his chin—"this is his profession."

"Undergrad?" I thought to myself.

Well, he did look somewhat young, but here I was, a grad student, closer to thirty than twenty. I still got carded everywhere I went, including the bar at TGIF.

"If I remember correctly, he's from Dallas. He plays here just about every other Friday," Lee said. "He usually closes the club down."

That was all the information I needed and with very little effort put forth on my part. Before the night was over, my plans for the next Friday were set in stone.

"I'm getting in the bathroom line," Lee said as Rodney ended his performance. "Can you grab me a bottle of water from the bar?" He asked over the crowd's applause.

"No problem."

We parted ways. The DJ put on Aaliyah's "One in a Million," and everyone that could, paired up for one last slow dance.

"Two bottled waters, please?" I asked the bartender.

"Seven even," he replied as he handed me the two bottles.

"I've got it," said a familiar voice.

Before it registered, a large dark-skinned hand reached over my shoulder and dropped a ten spot on the bar.

"Keep the change," said Rodney, beside me.

"Thanks," I barely managed.

"So which one is mine?" he replied with another sly wink as he leaned on the bar.

"Oh . . . these are . . . for me and my friend."

"Too bad," he said as the smile faded from his face. "I guess you should pay me back, then."

"Oh yeah. My bad."

I reached for my wallet, but he put a business card in my face.

"Just give me a ring sometime."

Reaching around my waist, he slipped the card into my back pocket.

"Later," he said, his smile back and brighter than before.

And then just like that, he was gone.

"You ready?" Lee asked, appearing out of nowhere again.

"Yeah," I answered quickly in a vain attempt not to seem startled by his sudden appearance.

"So you going to call him?" Lee asked as we walked to our cars in the parking lot.

"So you did see that?" I replied with a weak voice.

"The whole club saw it," he laughed. "You **were** just hit on by a local celebrity."

"Damn!"

"Man, cool out," he said with a little less amusement. "Not **that** many people were looking. And besides, this is Sin City," he explained, indicating the city with a wide gesture of his arms. "Anything goes."

I looked back so bewildered that I could feel the reddening of my checks.

"One of the main things I learned when I moved here from St. Louis is that the people here aren't quite as homophobic as those idiots back in the Midwest." He sighed, putting an arm around my shoulder. "There are a lot more amoral things to spew hellfire and brimstone over."

"Present company included?" I asked, looking doe-eyed and hopeful.

"Depending on who you ask, that would border on being hypocritical," he responded with a knowing glance and a crooked smile.

* * *

On my ride back home, I took out the card. Pretty professional. A photo of a sax on the right and a head shot of Rodney with a modest smile on the left.

Black Satin Productions.
Call 702-215-1262
for booking information or visit
www.blacksatinproductions.com

There was slightly smudged writing from fresh ink on the back—*702-214-1226*. It was also signed **Mr. Black Satin**. I gave in to my curiosity, pulled out my cell phone, and dialed the number on the back.

"Wassup, playboy?" asked Rodney's seductive voice on the other end.

"Do you know who you are talking to?" I asked.

"Somebody who owes me a drink."

"Hmmm. It sounds like you were very confident that I was going to call," I replied, regaining the wit that had abandoned me in the club.

"Well, I ain't called Mr. Black Satin for nothing."

"And who gave you that title?" I ask, beginning to rethink my decision to call him.

"I gave it to myself because I'm the smoothest, slickest man you'll ever meet."

I laughed out loud with surprise.

"Well, that is very modest of you," I replied when I caught my breath.

"Well, it ain't boasting when I run up on the sexiest lil' playboy in Sin City."

"Really?"

"Like you didn't already know that," he answered with a hint of a predatory growl.

"I plead the fifth on that, but I will admit you looked very nice tonight up on that stage."

"Really?" he said with a hint of surprise. "I usually only dress like that for my shows."

"Well, for the record, it was really working for me, especially the leather pants and boots."

"For real? So you like cowboys, hun?"

"Cowboys are the sexiest thing walking on three legs."

"Oh really." The amusement crept back into his voice. "So tell me this, are you a freak?"

"I'll tell you this much if you wearing that outfit you will be welcome into my bedroom anytime, day or night."

He howled with laughter.

"Nice to know I can make you laugh," I smiled into the phone.

"That ain't all you make me do," he said very deliberately.

"What else do I make you do?"

"I'll tell you about all that tomorrow when I swing by yo office on campus to take you to lunch."

He knew where I worked? So he'd been checking me out. That intrigued me more than anything else tonight.

"I'm sorry. Did I agree to a date?"

"Are you going to disagree?"

In that moment, I dug into my bag of witty retorts and came up empty.

"I didn't think so. I'll see you at noon."

ABSTRACT DESIRES

Abstract desires given concrete form.
An ivory smile set against ebony,
radiating a modest brilliance.
Shoulders that bear the heavens,
curving into a well-rounded back.
Sculpted calves of obsidian,
tempered bronze thighs.
A velvet voice that stills hearts
A golden touch which starts them again
Cure to my callousness
Balm to my bitterness
Heaven's gift, a true godsend.

07/18/00

Seron Wright Jr.

Seron 1.0

An hour later finds me leaving the second floor of Grandma Earlean's Westside two flat to spend time with Dad downstairs.

That's three interviews down. An infinite number more to go. Lord knows I love these people and appreciate the feelings being returned, but God, love is so high maintenance. I'm always worn-out to the point that I become very irritable with contacting and visiting all these people. I swear, not seeing or calling someone when you're the one who flew or drove hundreds of miles and half a day to come home must be the second highest federal offense in the land, right behind acts of terrorism. I sometimes wish I could broadcast the more public Disney-family-friendly aspects of my life via satellite and be done. Hell, I am a writer. Maybe I'll just put out a newsletter.

Thankfully, coming down the steps within the enclosed back porch gives instant access into the first-floor apartment. Grandma always calls their two flat a family building, so some doors are never locked when everyone is home. I hate waiting at the door. Dad hates getting up to answer the door. In light of that fact, it is amazing that we actually have visits. Perhaps love is stronger than laziness and lack of patience.

Through the kitchen and into the combined dining and living rooms.

"Aaww, there's my son," says my father, Seron Wright Sr., rising from his Yahoo! chess game.

He stands a couple inches taller than me.

"Well, you definitely eating good, Mr. Wright," I laugh while trying to fit my arms around his short muscular frame. "How you doing?" I ask, smothered by his hug.

I was definitely not lacking physical affection from a father figure coming up.

So much for that gay theory.

"Fine, and you, Mr. Wright?"

"I'm good."

We've been doing the "Mr. Wright and Mr. Wright" bit for so many years that no one finds it funny anymore. He and I just do it out of habit.

"You getting dark out there in the desert, but you looking good," he says, pulling away to look me over.

"Funny thing is, I'm hardly out in the sun," I reply while removing my jacket and spying the room for the nearest empty chair.

"Hmm, guess it doesn't take much, but I bet you like the weather."

"Warmer than Chicago year-round? You know it. I see why you and Grandma used to go two and three times a year."

Kind of already knowing the answer from our weekly phone calls, I ask, "So how are things with you?"

"I'm making it."

A few years back, he finalized his divorce from my stepmother, Trisha. A pretty amicable arrangement. They were only married for a few years. Nothing to fight over. The only children involved were hers. Amazingly, they needed paperwork to "just walk away." Honestly, it broke my heart like all divorces do. I'm pretty sure it is small in comparison to the heartbreak the two felt despite the fact that she left him, finally frustrated with their irreconcilable differences.

I pull one of the dining room chairs over and sit next to him, watching the chess game play out.

"We still talk, of course. You know her and the kids still coming to the church. They come around to visit in between services. There are no hard feelings on my side toward her," he said, half of his attention committed to the game.

"Well, from her e-mails to me, that's mutual. I guess if you have to . . . to . . ."

"Get a divorce?" he says, giving me a momentary sad glance.

"Yeah. If so, I guess that's the best you can hope for."

"You right about that, son. So that's that."

I can tell he is still disappointed, but thankfully, it doesn't get him down as much anymore. It definitely validates my life choice not to ever marry. It is the ugly side of the marriage coin—his divorce. If by some miracle I did marry and it ended in divorce, I'd never try again. That's not what I want for him, though. I know he sees the other side of the coin—my mom and my stepfather, a sort of dynamic duo, battling every obstacle as a team and coming out golden. I guess I don't want to do all that work for a gamble, a coin toss. I launch another sensitive topic that must be discussed in the air.

"So have you heard from your son?"

He tosses a hand in the air accompanied with a sigh.

"Terrence is all right."

I have another brother, Terrance, by my father with whom I have a somewhat estranged relationship. I take a good portion of the blame for that, considering the fact that I'm twelve years his senior. I let all my issues with being gay separate me from the people who love me. My relationship with my brother, Eric, is only a little bit better, mostly because we grew up in the same house well before I knew anything about being gay, let alone knowing to be ashamed.

"That's not what I asked," I reply. "I know he's all right."

To say that Dad's relationship with Terrence's mom isn't the greatest would be a gross understatement. In a small way, it contributes to the awkwardness that stands between us on the rare occasion that my brother and I see each other. It isn't that our parents keep us apart or even encourage distance. I guess, like my relationship with Eric and Regina, I worry about him being ashamed of his older gay brother. I never told him or his mom, but they know. And thanks to Dad, I know how Terrence feels about gay people—intolerant to say the least.

Let's see love undo that.

"He'll call when he wants something," Dad answers.

"So it is safe to assume you didn't call him either, then?"

He pretends to concentrate on his chess game.

"Well, I'm not the one to try and tell my father what to do, but you need to talk with your son," I say, acting as if I'm interested in the game.

"Yeah, we'll see," he replies, clicking his mouse vehemently.

Hmm, guess I know where I get my quiet avoidance coping strategies.

Rather than make this visit all about his failures and shortcomings or my being gay, which I still don't think he even acknowledges to himself, we make the unspoken compromise to turn to a more pleasant conversation.

"So how is the job? I'm surprised after the book deal that you are still working."

"It's cool. I guess it is just me being 60 percent practical and 40 percent scared of not having a steady monthly income."

"You get that from your grandfather. Even after retiring, he always had to be doing something."

The rest of that evening is filled with noneventful but casual, polite talk.

* * *

Walking to the car, I can just barely make out the Rock, the affectionate nickname the congregation uses for our church, the Rock of Salvation Missionary Baptist Church, where the proud pastor is blah blah blah. The only place or event I want to avoid as much as or maybe even more than the purpose of this visit, the hospital.

"Love of my life," Erykah Badu sings through my cell phone.

The special ring tone assigned to Rodney.

"Wassup, papi?" I ask, situating myself in the car.

"You, baby boi. Guess you still in the streets."

"Yeah. Just leaving my dad's."

"So have you at least called *him*?"

Him being Calvin.

"No . . . not yet. But I will catch up to him tomorrow during visiting hours."

"Don't punk out, nigga."

"Damn! You know I find it interesting that you are so supportive of me visiting my ex."

"That's 'cus I'm a man and secure with my shit."

"Oh, really. For all you know, I made the whole thing up as a cover to get up with my old flame."

"Nigga, please. We both know who that lil' hot booty belongs to."

"Hmmm."

"Don't act brand-new," he laughs.

After a few seconds of dead air, I let my guard down a bit.

"I miss you."

"Damn!" he exclaims. "You sure you alight?"

Just like that, the guard is back up and triple fortified. Ironically, I come to a red traffic light too.

"Yeah, I'm cool."

"All you got to do is say the word and I'm there."

"Naw, I'm cool. Just need some sleep. I'm sure I won't get much of that this weekend."

"You sound like you driving."

"Yeah. Taking the scenic route back to Mom's."

"You wanna talk 'til you get there?"

Hmm, that's the closest he's ever come to letting me know he misses me too, or is he checking up on me? Aside from his alpha male routine, he has never been really possessive or jealous, but we've never been apart at a distance like this nor for this long a time either.

The traffic light turns green.

"Cool," I reply, resuming to my late-night drive.

Not five minutes later, he is fast asleep. Normally, I would press buttons on the cell phone keypad to wake him, but the sound of his breathing is more like home to me than anything else I've felt in these past ten or twelve hours.

FRIDAY

Morning Glory

Awakening from blessed dreams.

Pale in comparison
to the vision before me.
Sunlight sweeping across
the still life that is your innocence.

Following the sweet rhythm.
Rising and falling.
Rising and falling.
A break.

And it begins again.

Tracing your outline,
through crumpled satin.
Closing in quietly,
attempting to inhale your essence.

A sudden flutter.
A look of bewilderment,
answered by assurance.
Contentment.

7/17/00
Seron Wright Jr.

Calvin

The sensation of Rodney's breath on my back and his hands caressing my stomach evaporates to be replaced by confusion and consciousness. It has been ages since I've woken up confused about where I was. Maybe it's the remodeling of my old bedroom. That thought stimulates sensual memory. That wasn't Rodney I slept with last night. Fully recalling who guest-starred in last night's dream, I release a groan of frustration and reach for my cell phone.

"You have reached West Suburban Hospital."

I don't really like people, but I really hate automated phone systems. After forcefully dialing 0 several times, trying in vain to avoid listening through the main, the sub, and sub-sub menu, I get the desired information.

"General visiting hours are from 10:00 a.m. until 8:00 p.m. Press 0 to reach switchboard or to be directed to the nurse's station."

I flip the phone closed and toss it to the side. Looking at the clock, it's only nine in the morning. I give in to temptation, lie back down, and chase the fading mental imagery brought on by last night's dreams. *The fog of memory is suddenly replaced with a more tangible herbal cloud . . .*

I nearly jumped out of my skin at his touch, not to mention the daze I had obviously been in for some time.

"Damn, you are full," laughed Calvin at my intoxicated state while he situated his arm around my shoulder. "What, you forgot I was sitting here next to you?"

We were side by side on the couch in front of the forty-inch-screen TV that was currently playing music videos courtesy of VH1 Soul.

"Man, shut the fuck up!" I retorted, moving his arm.

The air was a mix of two parts green—one part carbon dioxide and a hint of oxygen. To this very day, I get a little defensive when I'm high. Even more so when I'm drunk to boot, which was the case that night.

"I ain't no more fucked up than you!"

He leaned in closer with that sexy grin as big as Texas.

Calvin came to join our circle of friends not all too long after I did. He was introduced to us by Rich, one of the members who was dating him, well, trying to have him at least. The two met at a local barbershop where Calvin had just started working one early Saturday morning. After a few deliberate trips to Calvin's chair for the purposes of discerning the hot barber's tee, Rich confirmed what we all had been wondering. In the end, Calvin and Rich never made it to the bedroom, but the barber became a permanent fixture in our circle. I always found him kind of doable. Okay, very doable, but it would be messy to fool around with a friend who was once classified as a piece of trade for another friend. Very messy indeed.

"Okay. Now I know I'm fucked up," I admitted as I came to the realization that Calvin and I were the only people in Marcus and Maurice's living room. "I didn't even notice when everyone else left."

"They ran out for food and drinks," Calvin answered. "They asked you if you wanted anything and you said you was cool."

"Ohhhhh," I groaned as the world spun behind my closed eyes. "Shit!" Opening them rapidly really didn't help the situation.

"You okay, Lil' Magic?" he smirked.

Calvin had called me by a nickname other members of the circle long ago christened me with and then forgot.

He was the only one who said it from time to time. It had an odd quality that, I had to admit, made me warm on the inside. I never asked for confirmation of his intentions out of equal parts fear of his rejection and the jokes from the circle that my ego wouldn't ever survive.

"Yeah. Well, I will be in a minute," I answered, floundering to my feet.

My ten or so stumbling steps to the bathroom and my porcelain god of the evening took all eternity, infinity no higher. I got into the bathroom and closed the door. Opened a window. I braced myself with the sink and moved to kneel in worship when the door opened. From my vantage point, I recognized Calvin's shoes.

"Aw, man," he said with a voice full of disappointment.

He hooked his hands under my arms and lifted me to my feet.

His hands moved to my waist, and he walked me backward to the side of the tub. There he sat me down.

"Don't do that," he said as he knelt down from his height of five feet eleven until his dark caramel face met my own. "It will only make you feel worse."

I tried to avoid those eyes set in his perfectly groomed face by looking up and focusing on his short curly reddish brown Afro.

"You are a mess," he laughed.

"Fuck you!"

"You are even funnier when you all mad like that too. Like a lil' mad pit bull."

"Oh, so now I look like a dog. Yeah, this is making me feel better than throwing up ever could."

"You know that's not what I meant," he replied apologetically. "You are too damned sensitive. Cute, but too sensitive."

Sobriety gained a meager foothold at that last unexpected compliment. As he leaned in closer, it finally registered that he had never let go of my waist.

"They gonna be out for a while, you know," he let his voice drop down a bit on the scale.

Finally, against my better judgment, my eyes matched his gaze. Aww hell. I was stuck. He kissed me. There weren't any fireworks or anything earth-shattering, but it was nice. Like the long drink of ice-blue Kool-Aid you long for while walking home from the bus stop on a summer day in Chicago. No, not fireworks but very impressive. Not because of technique but because it was him. With one hand still on my waist, Calvin put the lid down on the toilet. He sat and pulled me onto his lap in a straddling position. He kissed me again while crushing me against his chest and pulling me into his lap so that I could feel his fully attentive manhood. He placed my arms around his shoulders. His hands traced my spine, seeking my butt. He gave the target a firm squeeze and released a lil' groan. His hands slid up a bit, seeking entry into my pants. We heard the sound of disturbed gravel, thanks to the open window. The rest of the circle had returned. His hands flew out of my pants.

"Feel better now?" he asked in a whisper as our foreheads rested on each other, our eyes closed.

"Ummm hmm."

It was all I could manage.

"Good."

He lightly slapped my ass, the signal for me to get up. He left the bathroom and closed the door behind him.

KISSING RAIN

Something like a summer rain,
though lighter,
akin to a light drizzle

Sunlight, illuminating
gray cumulus nimbus
from behind

Lovers moving at ease
through crystalline droplets,
Scattering sunshine into
seven shades of God's promises

No umbrellas
No raincoats
No inhibitions necessary

7/10/09
Seron Wright Jr.

REGINA

The sound of the doorbell brings me back to the waking world. I throw on the boxers by the side of the bed and make my way to the door. Opening the door, I'm met by the brilliant light of the sun and a beautiful tall stranger.

"Ummm. Is Regina here?" he asks.

Damn! Well, he looked a lil' young for me anyway.

"Let me see. Who is asking?"

"I'm her . . . uh . . . friend Jonathan."

"Oh. Yeah, you're her friend," I laugh.

Mental note: Stop provoking strangers, especially when they are black men that got me by at least one and a half feet and some seventy-odd pounds. At any rate lil' sis is doing good for herself. He *is* very nice to look at.

"I'm her brother Seron." I extend my hand.

"Nice to finally meet you."

"'Ron, I'm up here getting dressed," Regina calls down from upstairs.

"Okay!" I yell in response. "We'll be waiting for you in the living room."

I lead Jonathan into the living room, suddenly feeling a lil' naked. He sits on the couch. A little too comfortable for my taste, but he's obviously been here often enough. I can imagine him sitting in that same seat, only much more tense during his "interrogation." Mom and

Dad aren't mean people, but this is some guy with their lil' girl, so I know he got raked over some hot coals.

"You want something to drink?" I ask, walking toward my room for a shirt.

"No, thanks. I'm cool," Jonathan responds.

Well, he's hot and polite. She did real good. There is just one thing I need to check that I know the parental squad missed. Walking to my room, I can check out his reflection in the open swinging glass door that divides the dining room and the kitchen. Hmm . . . well, he's not watching me or, more importantly, my ass. Not that I'm absolutely irresistible, but I know I tend to attract guys like him. Big guys like him seem to get off at the prospect of a compact and cute boy like myself. Guess it makes them feel a bit more like the alpha male or something. Whatever the case, he didn't set off my gaydar before, but now I'm fairly certain Regina won't be dealing with no drama from a DL bisexual brother, dating her while secretly trying to get up in another man's pants.

"So Regina said you were in the reserves or something, right?" I ask, coming back in to turn on the TV and sit in the armchair.

"National Guard going on two years," he responds.

"That's cool. So where you going from there?"

"To be honest, I'm considering college. Kind of hard to keep up with Regina, though." He laughs. "But seriously, I've always had a thing for engineering. I just wasn't feeling college right out of high school."

"Well, I can understand that. And it's not like you graduated and sat on your butt either," I say, my fingers working the TV remote.

I channel-surf past cartoons, cooking shows, and Court TV. Finally, I stop on HGTV.

"Regina talks about you a lot," Jonathan says out of the blue.

I visibly try not to blush at that statement.

"She said you did undergrad and grad."

"Uhh . . . yeah," I reply, recovering my composure.

"And that is how you got out to Vegas, right?"

"Well, there were a couple of things—the job, school, wanting to see something different." I fight the urge to roll my eyes with that last statement.

God, how long am I going to keep telling that "wanting to see something different" lie? It's partially true, but I was running *from* more things than I was running *to*.

"Yeah, I get that. I get to travel some too, but I haven't got out of the country yet."

Hmm, a brother that has been off his own block and has international travel aspirations. Is it too soon to call him brother-in-law?

"You know, I'd love to go overseas, but I want to see a lot more of the US first," I interject, turning to face him directly.

"Where would you like to go after seeing everything over here?" he asks, still very comfortable from my vantage point.

"I'm thinking Paris, Cairo, Milan."

True answers but still fishing for the OGTs (obviously gay traits).

"Cool, cool. Not big on Paris and hadn't thought about Milan, but I feel you on Cairo. I'd love to make a tour of Africa. Hit up Cairo, Cape Town, and a few places in between." Jonathan's eyes light up at the prospect of his future adventures.

I begin to flip through the channels again in an attempt to be attentive but not too taken in.

"A couple friends of mine online have done it, and they always talk about this connection you feel in the motherland. It's like coming home from what they say. Like just knowing that you are where you belong. Granted everyone isn't happy to see us over there but everyone over here isn't either," he adds, relaxing more into his seat.

Oh man, the boy knows geography and is socially conscious, nationally and internationally. I think I'm in love. I will admit Regina had us all a little worried a few years back. She was hanging out with guys who didn't appear to have her best interest in mind, to say the least.

"Yeah, that is how a lot of people I know described the trip. Man, I have to be honest," I say, looking at him very deliberately. "I trust my sister's judge of character and my parents' interrogation, but it wasn't until meeting you now that I have to say I'm as cool as can be about you and my sister dating."

Jonathan stiffens up ever so slightly. That obviously knocked him off his pivot foot. Thankfully, Regina comes down the stairs at just that point. Lord, she ages me every time I go without seeing her for long periods of time. She didn't get much taller than me, but she got a few more modest curves. Her love life aside, we just couldn't get into Regina's head and figure out what she wanted for herself in regard to her future. Now she is working toward becoming a pediatric nurse, a fulfilling career path she picked for herself. I'm so proud of her, but while I look at how she has grown and matured, it still adds to my own years.

"Hey, I must have been asleep when you got back in last night," she says, crossing the room to hug me.

"Yeah, it was pretty late."

"Okay, so did he pass the test?" she laughs, moving to sit next to Jonathan who smiles nervously.

"Yeah, he's cool. So what ya'll getting into today?" I say, returning his smile.

"Lunch, mall, maybe the movies," she answers with a casual toss of her hand.

"Mall? What, you getting yo *fit* for tonight?" I laugh.

"Yeah," she chuckles.

"Girl, you know I know about Friday nights in college. I still couldn't imagine being in college in the city, though."

"Yeah, having the option to club versus a college party is cool," Jonathan chimes in.

I hear the sound of my phone coming from my room.

"I guess my day is officially getting started," I say, getting up.

"Did you catch up to any of your friends yet?" Regina asks.

"I left a few messages. That's probably one of them now. I'll call back after I shower."

"Okay, well, we should be on our way out, then."

"We'll see who makes it in the latest tonight then." I laugh.

"Nice meeting you," says Jonathan, extending his hand.

"You too."

A Dreadlocked Mystery

About thirty minutes later, I'm in the shower surrounded by steam and the sounds of music playing at random from my MP3 player, trying to wash off the grime of yesterday and the awkwardness of feeling fairly certain that my sister knows I'm gay. We've never really talked about it or how she feels. I wonder if she told Jonathan. Before I get too committed to that line of thought, Foxy Brown's "Candy" comes on.

"Ohhh, that's my shit!"

My body is moving in the shower, but my mind is grooving at a party in Atlanta.

The circle made annual trips to Hot-Lanta for Black Gay Pride every MLK weekend. Of course, I told everyone we were going down for parties that they assumed were straight affairs. In reality, it was a weekend of people watching, posing, posturing, shopping, clubs, parties, drinks, weed, and men. It hardly had a basis in reality. It was all about working a glamour as I called it. Dressing up and putting on airs under the guise of being the you that you couldn't, wouldn't dare to be back home. Who knew it took so much effort to just be yourself? But that wasn't the case with US.

I was the most effeminate of our group and the runt of the pack, but far from being the biggest "girl" of any one party, let alone the weekend. We all pretty much dressed and acted the same way we would have on the streets back home. We were spectators of a sort, engaging in the party experience but watching "the chase." On occasion, I got caught up in the chase myself. Equal parts loneliness and lust acted as my motivators. I did my best to be seen but not appear to be putting forth the effort. I always got fixated on at least one guy. Never the cock of the walk, mind you. I equated myself to the predator who sought out the lone gazelle that strayed away from the pack. I continuously broke all the rules by hoping to make some **meaningful connection** in a setting where 85 percent of the guys were only seeking one-night stands—the more anonymous the better. At most, it got me a hot dance partner for a few minutes.

I followed my usual pattern and danced closer and closer to my intended target. Then beside him. All the while, I watched his eyes to determine if he seemed remotely interested. Stalker mode fully engaged. One particular night, "he" manifested in the person of a mocha grande, mahogany colored, dreadlocked mystery. On top of a fairly attractive face and a physique visible even under alternating red, blue, and yellow club lighting, he was moderately dressed in a simple long-sleeved dark thin gray sweater, pressed straight-legged charcoal jeans, and casual black Prada slip-on shoes. My mating dance caught his attention. Our eyes locked, and we danced closer to each other until we were literally on top of each other. Our upper torsos and midsections melded together to the rhythm of Beyonce's "Baby Boy."

"So you here by yourself?" he whispered into my ear while lightly gripping my waist to pull me closer to him.

"Naw," I replied as I reached up and put my arms around his neck. "Me and my guys came down together."

"Cool."

"My name is Seron."

"Uh, Dwayne," he answered.

"So I guess you not from here either, huh?" I asked.

His grip loosened.

"Just here for the weekend," he said absentmindedly.

"Where you from?" I pressed unintentionally.

He pulled away a bit.

"St. Louis."

"You ever make your way up to Chicago?"

"Naw. Not much," Dwayne replied.

"Okay."

At that moment, I finally noticed that his eyes had been roaming around the party, obviously searching for something or anyone else.

"Well, it was nice meeting you," he said gently but swiftly working himself free of my embrace without making eye contact.

"Um . . . okay."

He disappeared farther onto the crowded dance floor.

Another nice put-down for my already full-grown collection. A mixed blessing in retrospect. At the time, Atlanta was the STD, HIV, and AIDS capital of Black Gay America during the off-peak season. Pride brought in even more variety. We always made the joke, "Don't take anything back home that you didn't buy in the mall." I made my way to the bar, trying to wash down the rejection. I did my best to contain my lil' hurt feelings for the time being and got back onto the dance floor.

By the third year, it was an accepted pattern that I would get so drunk that I'd miss the majority of at least one night of partying, usually sick in a bathroom. It wasn't until Calvin joined us on the trip that the pattern was broken.

The hot water starts to get cooler, bringing me back to life. It occurs to me that I haven't heard from Rodney this morning yet.

WHERE MY GIRLS AT

"Ya got yo, boy Rod. Leave a message and I'll hit you back."

I flip the phone closed and toss it into the passenger seat.

"Okay. That was call number 4," I say to myself, speeding east on 290, making my way to meet the girls for lunch.

When was the last time I invoked the rule of three? Seron's dictionary defines the rule of three as follows: calling these knuckleheaded niggas three times and leaving three reliable messages before deleting their numbers out of the phone so as to prevent me from further playing myself and then leaving them alone altogether. Not ready to delete Rodney just yet, but IF I HAVE TO CALL HIM AGAIN TODAY, THE MESSAGE WILL BE TO HAVE EVERY PAIR OF YO DAMN DRAWERS OUT OF MY PLACE BY THE TIME I TOUCH DOWN IN VEGAS! Okay, a bit extreme, I'll admit, but why can't niggas just be where they are supposed to be? Where they are supposed to be = where I want them to be.

* * *

"There's my husband," calls Yasmine, one of my four friends, as I exit the elevator into the Signature Room at the top of the John Hancock building.

Yasmine always says that she feels so close to me that we must have been lovers in another lifetime. I usually reply that she must have driven me to date men in this one. She jumps up from the table, startling a few of the other customers, and runs over to me.

"Man, it is good to see you too."

I barely have the air to respond. Yasmine surprises me with a bear hug that one wouldn't expect from a 5'4" 120 lb. woman.

"My favorite African American male author!" exclaims Jordan, using a name she christened me with back in college.

She has always been the biggest fan of my writing. Weaving her petite body in between the other giggling customers, she meets us halfway back to the table.

"Yo ass ain't that damn famous for me to be jumping up from this table like that!" laughs Shawn. "Come over here and give me my hug."

"Oh, we are so proud of you," says Donna, the final of the four hugging me.

Staring at four of my best friends, two from college and two from as far back as high school, I see that they are as different as the Cosmo, Apple Martini, White Russian, and Raspberry Stoli they have before them. Shawn and Donna are on the thick side. Shawn and Jordan are lighter skinned, while Donna and Yasmine are darker. Donna and Jordan favor natural hair in the form of a short Afro and shoulder-length dreads respectively. Shawn and Yasmine lean toward the "bone straight," dark and lovely section of the Beauty Supply Store. Each of them is a successful African American woman in her own right, in professions ranging from investment banking to educational administration. Until a birthday party I had some years back, I always had a horrible experience with mixing friends. These four, despite their diverse physiques and their nearly infinite number of less-visible differences, mix easier than rum and Coke and don't require me to play the part of social adhesive. A rare quality in my various circles of friends, especially those composed of females or gay males.

Glimpsing out of the window, taking in the clear sunlit view of the city below us, I wonder if they know how vital their various expressions of love and acceptance are to my being the person I am, not to mention my just *being* here today. Four pillars of my sanity. I know that I was blessed, beyond measure, to have a family that loves me and, to a degree, understands and accepts me for who I am, but it is always special to find people who aren't obligated to love you for tangible yet superficial blood ties. Maybe love isn't all too high a maintenance after all. Maybe.

"Man, we missed yo narrow lil' ass," says Shawn. "Don't you ever go that long without visiting us again."

"Girl, calm down," says Yasmine, coming to my defense. "He ain't even made his drink order yet."

"Last I checked, planes fly out of Midway and O'Hare to Vegas all day, every day," I shoot back, reaching for the drink menu.

"Hmmm, but will you have any space for us? You got a lot going on with this boy you shackin' up with," Shawn replies, stirring her drink with a straw.

"Awww, hell naw," laughs Donna, hiding her face behind a napkin. "You done robbed the cradle?"

A hint of crimson creeps across the surface of my usual Reese's Cup brown complexion.

"Yes, he did and with an aspiring musician," Shawn continues just before sipping on her drink. "What does he play again?" she asks, turning to me.

"Saxophone and piano," I mumble, shifting in my seat, desperately seeking the waiter.

"Ohhh, a jazz man," Donna giggles, patting me on the back.

"Wait a minute now, ladies," says Jordan, with a snap of her fingers. "Ain't nothing wrong with having a boy toy."

"All I want to know is why I ain't heard nothing about this *boy toy* 'til now," says Yasmine, crossing her arms, pretending to be jealous.

"Can I get you something to drink?" asks a voice from over my shoulder.

I'm saved by the waiter.

"Excuse me, waiter," asks Yasmine, fishing something out of her purse, "but can you please take our picture?"

"No problem," the waiter answers, reaching for her camera.

"I just figured that it is so rare that we have the chance to get together these days that I'd better document the event," she explains to the rest of us as we all huddle in together.

I love these girls and the fact that they can all get along like no other four black women I know. That is until they all band together to let me have it.

* * *

Three hours, four cocktails, and one round-trip up and down Michigan Avenue later . . .

"It is so weird to be carrying a Macy's bag instead of a Marshall Field's bag," I think out loud in the car, alone with Yasmine.

"Thank you soooo much for the ride to my car," says Yasmine, rubbing her feet.

"That's what you get for wearing those brand-new shoes right out of the store." I laugh.

"I was breaking them in!"

"Yeah, whatever, Ms. Manolo Blahnik. You wore them 'cause you was trying to be cute."

"Well, I don't recall you walking into the store with those, Mr. Cole Haan." She scowls in the direction of the new shoes on my feet.

"True, but the difference is that *my* feet don't hurt."

"Shut up!" Yasmine playfully slaps my cheek. "It was so good playing catch up in person." She leans in, following up the abuse with a kiss. "You would think for as much as we talk every week on the phone and through instant messengers we wouldn't have anything to gag about in person."

"So is everyone still planning to show for my mom's dinner?" I ask, trying to avoid the subject of the hospital, visitation hours, and Calvin especially. Based on the conversation at lunch, I now know that she hadn't informed the other girls why I was actually in town. Despite my closeness to all of them, Yasmine usually got the most complete disclosure.

"Boy, we was sold when you said food," she laughs while playfully hitting me on the shoulder.

Why does she always have to hit? Does she know how freakishly strong she is?

She hesitates for a moment.

"So you going to see him tomorrow?"

"Yeah," I release a sigh, looking away from Yasmine.

"Ron. You came all this way, and he needs to see you."

I unhook my seat belt and turn to grab Yasmine's shopping bags from the backseat.

"Look, you grown. You know what to do. Give a ring if ya'll get into something good tonight." She slides out of the car, shoes and bags in hand. "Bye, husband."

"Later, Yasmine." I wave in response.

M & M

The flow of traffic and a melancholy mood carries me back west on the Eisenhower. Brian McKnight's "Anytime" comes on, and I can't change the radio quick enough. Once again, my treacherous memory conspires with the music, transporting me to a much darker time.

All in an instant, the early evening sky is replaced with a teary nighttime scene. Still traveling on the expressway but speeding east at breakneck velocity. Demanding answers and absolution from a god who appears to have closed the heavens on me. Contemplating pills and casting myself in the role of Sleeping Beauty sans the prince who would come with a kiss, breaking this gay curse. A fractured mind in the guise of absolute clarity offers a deadly resolution. The tears dry up forever that night as I purchase the pills and lie down for what I hope and pray will be my last mortal sleep.

The sounds of Three 6 Mafia's proclamation to "Stay Fly" come piping through my cell phone, snatching me back to reality.

"Shello," comes Maurice's voice on the other end of the line.

A greeting popular within our circle.

"Hey," I respond, pulling myself together.

"I touched down at O'Hare about a half an hour ago, but Marcus isn't due for another two hours."

Maurice is originally from the northwest suburbs of Chicagoland. Marcus came to us from Georgia. Maurice and Marcus, or M & M as I often referred to them, were the nucleus of the circle. They lived in Chicago for years as roommates, but the city got a little small for all of us. Maurice moved to Manhattan, and Marcus went to DC. I understood the desire for something bigger, and I took their relocation as my cue to be adventurous as well. A year later, I followed suit and made my way West.

"Well, I can ride out that way and wait with you," I answer back, checking the time and mentally calculating my ETA.

"Cool, I got a seat saved for you at the bar."

My drive is slowed to a crawl due to the Friday-evening rush-hour traffic. While the car rolls along at a snail's pace, my mind moves a mile a minute.

It had been months since Calvin and I made out in the bathroom, and nothing came of it. He did get more affectionate as far as things like hugging me when we all met up. To my surprise, I easily returned his affection. Either action was abhorrent among the rest of the circle who almost never even shook hands. But there wasn't a romantic feel to Calvin's touch, though. I even came to see him just as I saw M & M, as the older, somewhat overly protective brother I never had. Okay, I guess I thought overly protective because of my occasional bouts of "little man's disease," feeling the need to do everything just as well as if not better than my larger counterparts. It was an unspoken rule within the circle that he and I would always sit together on the couch watching TV, in the movie theater, in the car, even on the plane when we all traveled together to Atlanta that fateful fourth year.

As always, we'd party until about an hour before the sun came up. Roll up one more good smoke on the way to get a late-night snack from the Waffle House. Upon arriving back to the hotel, everyone would fall into the sweetest alcohol and marijuana-induced sleep. There were almost always four of us, which worked out to two sharing a bed. Maurice and Marcus always shared, which automatically put me in the bed with the fourth traveler. Despite us all being gay men and a decent mix of tops, bottoms, and versatile guys, it was like sleeping with your brother.

Anyway, one morning, like most, we all assumed our usual sleeping arrangements and passed out. I rolled over in my sleep, and my face became buried in Calvin's bare chest. I didn't even notice until I had trouble breathing. I moved to roll back over, and Calvin's hand caught my shoulder. I wasn't sure if his eyes were open because mine were still closed. His hand slid to the small of my back, and he pulled me closer to him. I could feel his warm breath on my forehead just before he moved his body down, brought his face to mine, his lips on top of mine.

"Ummm," he grumbled.

It was just a light kiss on the lips.

"Where you going, Lil' Magic?" he whispered in my ear.

"Just rolling over," I murmured in response.

"Hmm."

He released his hold just enough for me to twist around within his arms. His hands lightly gripped my stomach, and he pulled me back into the sweetest spooning position. He kissed me lightly on the cheek.

"You cool now?"

"Yeah, this is better," I responded.

In minutes, we had both fallen back asleep. I knew M & M woke up before us, but they never said anything about Calvin and I sleeping like lovers. Maybe they knew I'd get defensive. Maybe they expected our coupling. Maybe Calvin told them about the bathroom. Whatever the case, Calvin and I were sure they knew there was something going on. He and I didn't speak of it, even to each other. With unspoken agreement, we got to be even more physical, at least in friendly gay settings.

The rest of that trip, Calvin would walk with his arm around my shoulders. We'd dance together on the floor, but hardly very sexually. We slept together in an embrace from that trip on. He and I never had privacy due to the sleeping arrangements, but I'm sure we would have had sex that first weekend if we did. Regardless, those were three of the most peaceful nights of sleep I'd ever had in my life.

* * *

"Well, I see you doing better with that fear of heights," laughs Marcus hours later, joining me at the picture window of the suite he and Maurice checked into on the eighteenth floor of the W Hotel.

"Yeah, it's one of the things I've gotten better with," I reply as we overlook the Friday-evening traffic on Lake Shore Drive and a relatively calm Lake Michigan.

"Yes, I see." He casts a glance at my shopping bags from the outing with the girls. "Your fashions have come up too, sir."

"Well, I have M & M consulting to thank for that."

"True," says Maurice, stepping out of the bathroom in his evening party attire, a form-fitting black Penguin tee, blue jeans, and white K-Swiss. "Too bad those culinary lessons didn't stick."

"Hey now, I picked up on all that home improvement, computer and car maintenance stuff." I laugh in response. "Besides my husband finding prospects have yet to suffer *and* the menu at Chez Ron's has added a few more items."

M & M were the proverbial jacks-of-all-trades. My fathers taught me a lot, but for some reason, it was actually fun to learn with and from my guys. In my eyes, they could do just about anything. Once, they said they were going to lay their own hardwood floors. I was like, whoa, okay. I came back a week later to find lumber all over the place. About a month and a half later, the floors were so good you would have thought they paid Home Depot an arm and a leg a piece. It got to the point that if they told me, on Saturday, that they were building the *Star Ship Enterprise*, I would have expected to see it hovering above the house by that following Tuesday. It was all those hands-on skills and more masculine interests that made it hard for even me to believe they were gay despite some of our similar tastes in men.

"So how is Calvin?" Maurice asks while Marcus takes his turn in the bathroom.

"I haven't seen him yet," I answer while rummaging through my shopping bags, looking for my own party wear.

"Are you serious? You have been here since Thursday." He looks on in mild shock.

"I got here late Thursday and have been running around to see—" I say, purposely not looking up from my task.

"Uh-huh," he says, cutting me off so swiftly that I finally look at him. "Don't forget who you talking to. You obviously just tripping off old shit. So just say so."

I shot him a quick grimace on my way to the mirror with my purposed clubbing outfit.

"Hmmm. I'll just take that as confirmation," says Marcus, leaving the bathroom. "Tonight you gonna take yo punk ass in that bathroom and get dressed. Tomorrow you are going to the hospital with us."

On my way into the bathroom, my cell phone rings. I move to answer it, but irritation takes over, and I decide to get dressed instead.

My First Time with a Barber

A few drinks, a couple blunts, and a line full of queens, DL boys, and "homo fem thugs" later, we're in the Prop House. We see a few familiar faces but mostly familiar types—the young club bunnies on the floor battling the voguing queens for the attention of the more masculine men standing along the walls, who eye them like so many pieces of meat. The divas drift in and out of the smoke and flashing lights, posing and poochin'. We aren't really into the usual people watching tonight. Our reunion, among other things, has us on a high that carries us onto the dance floor already vibrating to the beat of Joe Budden's "Fire."

I must be as cute as I feel because I'm not short on dance partners at all. Or more likely, it is the fact that I've been away from Chicago so long that to all the regular club heads I appear to be fresh meat. Either way, I feel the cramp in my side from dancing out of my shirt and down to my wifebeater, a sign that I'm enjoying myself.

Why did I cut my dreads? I think while wiping the sweat out of my eyes and off my close-cropped head.

I go to the bar for an overpriced bottle of water.

"Three fifty," the muscular, honey brown, topless bartender says with a smile.

I hand him a five-dollar bill.

"Keep the change," I reply, returning the smile and blowing him a kiss.

I catch the sudden sensation of a vibration in my pants. With a huff into the air, I ignore the cell phone that is almost desperate for my attention. I find a seat on one of the couches as the waves of intoxication bowl me over.

Watching all these gay men in their natural habitat reminds me of all the effort that goes into nights like this—the shopping, the grooming, the *getting full* (of alcohol, marijuana, etc.) on the way to the club, all to see and to be seen. To be fair, there are a few instances of partying just to be partying, but in a lot of cases, there is the futile search for love and acceptance from a majority of people who don't fully love and accept themselves. Rather than dwell on the present sad reality, I close my eyes with a judgmental frown and follow my high down the rabbit hole to find myself years earlier with the circle, sitting around and watching movies at Calvin's place.

"Okay, this is late," said Maurice, waking up as the credits began to roll. "We are not spending another night in the house. We need to pull it together and hit the club."

"Sounds like a plan," said Marcus.

"I'm with that," said Calvin, looking to me.

"Well, I guess I won't be making it to church on time tomorrow, if at all." I laughed.

"Cool," said Marcus. "We'll roll back to the crib and get dressed."

I stood up to get my coat and noticed an unsightly imperfection in the mirror.

"Wassup, Lil' Magic?" asked Calvin.

"The kids are going to let me have it. I'm in desperate need of a lining."

"Man, you got an in-house barber right here. I can line you up with time enough for you to run home and change."

"We'll just all meet at the club, then," said Maurice, on his way out of the door behind Marcus.

A few minutes later, I sat in a chair in the kitchen listening to Twista's "Lavish" over the hum of the liners Calvin used on my head. From my point of view, I could see his waist sway a little to the beat. He never did this for me, but the experience was the same as with any other barber. It always amazed me how a man—whose big rough hands that lift hundred pound weights three to four times a week, handle the rock every Saturday morning, and, if necessary, beat down other niggas on the rare occasion—could use those same hands to touch my face and guide my head so gently with very little verbal direction. Like many of my other barber sessions, he just had to get so close that **he** rubbed up against my arms and shoulders. Thankfully, he appeared to be concentrating so intently that he didn't notice that I was trying to determine if he was **excited** or not.

"You know, I can do this for you on the regular," he said, finishing up.

"Do what?"

"Line you up for free," he answered as he put the mirror to my face.

"Naw." I wave the offer off while examining my reflection. "That's okay."

"Man, why is it always so hard for you to accept stuff from people?" He sighed, brushing the loose hair off me.

I removed the bath towel he used to keep the hair off my shirt and gave it to him.

"I just . . . Man, I don't know."

I reached for my wallet.

"Your money's no good here," he laughed and put up one hand to stop me.

He brushed my loose hair off his wifebeater.

I stood on my toes and gave him a kiss on the cheek.

"What was that about?" he smiled, a little surprised.

Look at him blush.

"Well, you said my money was no good, so I wanted to give you something."

Calvin looked down and away for a second. Then he rolled up the bath towel that he was still holding. In one swift motion, he looped it around my waist and pulled me into him.

He stooped down to face me and whispered, "I think I owe you some change."

He planted a kiss on my lips. His tongue glazed my bottom lip before seeking out my own. In the midst of all this, he released his hold on the towel and snatched at the back of my shirt. He pulled it up over my head and leaned back against the wall smiling.

"What?" I asked, feeling a lil' exposed.

I've always felt self-conscious about my little body.

With one hand, he pushed the dreads away from my face.

"Just checking out my handiwork," he said.

He looked down and away again.

All right, nigga, this game has lasted longer than a monopoly marathon, I thought to myself. Time to cash in my property, the houses, hotels, and all four railroads.

"And you needed to take off my shirt to do that?" I asked him while closing the gap between us until I could tell that he was just as **excited** as I was.

"Damn, Lil' Magic!" he sighed, rubbing up and down my bare arms.

"What's wrong?" I asked, forcing him to make eye contact.

"Nothing's wrong," he answered, just barely catching his breath. "Everything is cool."

His hands moved from my arms and to the small of my back. We went in for another kiss, which he cut short. He led me to the door of the bedroom. On the one hand, I was hoping that this was going where I had secretly longed for us to when we first met. On the other, I was terrified by the fact that I hadn't taken any of my usual presex precautions.

God, I could really mess this up, I thought. Damn my aggressive ass.

Calvin turned to see that I'd stopped short. He took my hand. Walking backward, he led me to the bedside where he sat and positioned me in between his legs. With his hands on my waist, he pulled my chest in to meet his lips. I arched my back and contemplated what the ceiling looked like behind my closed eyelids.

Calvin lightly kissed each of my nipples. He moved down to my belly button, all the while massaging the small of my back and my shoulder blades. He parted my legs with one foot, then slipped in the other and lowered me onto his lap, with my knees on the bed. Sweeping the hair away from one side of my neck, he went in for a taste and decided to stay. His tongue swept down and under my chin, following the path to the other side of my neck.

Finally, Calvin came up for air. Looking me in the eye, a sly grin appeared on his face.

"Whooops," he chuckled as he fell back onto the bed, pulling me down on top of him.

The kissing and back-rubbing began again but only long enough to throw me off balance while he made the next calculated move—the predictable "roll over with me, finally ending up on my back" move. Predictable, yes, but I was so gone at that point who gave a fuck. Like the countless others before him and very few after, he balanced himself above me on his elbows while kissing me.

I HATE BEING HANDLED LIKE GLASS!

Taking matters into my own hands quite literally, I wrapped my arms under his and around his shoulders to pull him down on top of me.

"I love the feel of you on top of me," I moaned into his ear just before sampling his neck.

He relaxed a bit until his groin met mine, and then he fully treated me to his man weight.

Calvin exhaled a sigh of satisfaction.

His hand slid down my side and into my pants.

When did he undo my pants? *I thought.*

He rolled slightly onto his side, pulling me up a bit with him until he could fully palm half of my ass in his hand. We moaned in unison as he worked my pants down and away a little more.

In between nibbling on my nipples and teasing me with his fingers, he whispered, "What you wanna do, Lil' Magic?"

It was far from the hardest decision I ever had to make.

"Hmmmm . . . I want to do this."

"Are you sure?" he asked to my surprise.

"Yesss," I responded again, rubbing the back of his head.

Trying not to move too enthusiastically, he sat up and pulled my pants off completely, including my socks and underwear in the process, and looked down on me with a predatory stare while he slowly undid his pants.

The vibration on my leg wakes me. It takes a second to register that I'm still in the club. Reluctantly, I take the phone out of my pocket. One text message.

Wassup playboy?

"Hmmm . . ."

Two voice mail messages.

"You are full," laughs Maurice, coming to sit next to me.

"Yeah," I say, still contemplating on giving in to wanting to hear Rodney's voice.

Fat Man Scoop shouting "If you got a twenty-dollar bill, throw yo hands up!" reminds me that using a phone in a loud club is futile. My desires were cut short by the expected assortment of excuses from Rodney, lacking a sense of remorse or responsibility.

"I didn't hear my phone."

"I just got your messages."

"I was working."

Just fill in the _____.

"Ya'll ready?" asks Marcus, finding Maurice and I half-asleep.

"Yeah," we reply in a unanimous sleepy sigh.

Leaving the club, we make a quick pit stop at Maxwell's off Roosevelt and the Dan Ryan expressway for a late-night polish. Rather than trek all the way back to Mom's, I spend the night on the couch in M & M's suite, attempting, in vain, to catch hold of the earlier dream. All I accomplish is making myself more lonely for Rodney. Thankfully, sleep and exhaustion takes hold relatively quick.

SOUTHERN COMFORT

It begins, at the neck
An ivory spread from
here to Texas

Brewed, blended to perfection
with pleasant politeness
200 percent proof grain
fermented to sensuous satisfaction

The beauty of the
Carolinas personified
Southern hospitality
given liquid form

Chocolate ambrosia
fueling the heart's fire
Dark nectar
soothing the soul with ease

Warm sunlight methodically
massaging tense hips
Rippling river waters
crashing against inner shores

Sheltered in the shadow
of a mighty Oak
Caressed in loving branches
Bathed by beautiful breezes

Lush clouds,
bringing summer rains
Cooling my lips

3/01/01

Seron Wright Jr.

SATURDAY

COMMITMENT... YIKES!

I wake up too abruptly to recall what I dreamt about. I lie there long enough to hear that M & M haven't gotten up yet. It takes a minute for my eyes to focus on my cell phone's clock. Another three missed calls, each accompanied by a voice mail according to the phone display—6:53 a.m. Wonderful. I still have a little snooze time. Besides, it's 4:53 a.m. Vegas time. He's still asleep anyway. I roll back over and pull the covers over my head.

"Morning," he said while pulling me closer to him as we lay in the bed the next morning.
"Hmmm," I moaned in response.
"Is that a good 'hmmm' or a bad 'hmmm'?"
"Definitely a good 'hmmm,'" I chuckled into Calvin's chest.
For a while, we just laid there. I didn't want to ask any of the typical questions the insecure "girl" would ask. I choked down my feelings and moved to sit up on the side of the bed. Calvin's long arm was wrapped around my waist as he got himself in an upright position behind me. He kissed the back of my neck and then moved to my ear.
"I wish I didn't have to let you go," he whispered.

My body stiffened with the rise of my emotional defenses.

"What was that about?" he asked with a nervous laugh.

"Nothing," I sighed while gently trying to work my way out of his arms. He responded with a more firm hold.

"Come on, man," he said, a little agitated. "After all that, you still won't drop your guard around me."

I just sat there in silence, determined not to be the bad guy, waiting until he let me go.

"Okay, look," he began. "I don't know what is up with you, but I'll put myself out there and tell you that I've wanted to be with you since the first day I met you, and not just sexually. I mean, I had a great time last night, no doubt, but I like being around you. You just make me feel good. Maybe there is a better way to say it, but that's how I feel. I was hoping that you felt the same way."

I still sat there waiting to be released. What seemed an eternity later, Calvin breathed a sigh of disappointment and slowly let go of me. He got up and went to the bathroom. Each footfall resounded my rejection of his emotional out pouring. I was dressed and out of the door before I could hear water making contact with water. I didn't want to stick around long enough for either of us to change my mind. Racing home, I saw that it was still early enough for me to make it to church.

"Better late than never, I suppose . . ."

"Okay, time to return to the land of the living," calls Marcus.

"What time is it?" I groan, my head still buried under the covers.

"Almost eleven," he responds.

"What's for breakfast?" I ask.

"We feeling a lil' lazy and a lil' grand this fine morning," says Maurice, coming from the bathroom. "We'll be reviewing the room service selection."

He tosses a menu my way.

"Then we are going to pull it together and get over to the hospital," Marcus adds.

I bury my head under the covers again.

A couple of hours later, we're in my rental car, making our way through the recently gentrified Austin neighborhood to the hospital.

"It is always funny to come home after so long and see how things have changed," I think out loud.

"Yeah," replies Maurice from the passenger seat. "New York has been cool, but every now and again, I consider moving back."

"Same with DC," says Marcus from the backseat. "They don't have Chicago's food for one thing."

At that moment, I burp.

"Damned late-night polish runs," I sigh.

We all laugh at that as we pull into the hospital parking lot.

I hadn't hung out so tight with a crew of guys since my high school days and the fellowship of my fraternity in college. In those two cases, I made the horrid mistake of distancing myself because of my interpersonal issues. Running with Maurice and Marcus was like a second chance at a male adolescence that I didn't allow myself to experience fully the first time around. The difference being, we have bigger allowances, much better toys, and a lot more drugs, sex, and clubbing. A mustard seed more of self-acceptance didn't hurt either. It was a little weird, but I actually felt my most masculine around them. Hell, I even came to enjoy watching sports. Baseball even! Nothing short of an act of God. I felt more at home in their presence than almost anywhere else. That, without a doubt, was why I felt a since of abandonment when they moved. Of course, I would never admit it to anyone.

As we approach the front desk inside the hospital, someone grabs my wrist. I swiftly turn around, fist locked and ready to fly. The untrusting Negro in me.

"Wassup, playboy?"

"Rodney!"

"Rodney!" exclaim M & M in unison.

There he is, wearing a grin of accomplishment.

"I know this is crazy, me showing up like this," he laughs while releasing my wrist to pull me into a bear hug, "but I did try to let you know I was coming. Why didn't you answer yo phone?"

We separate enough to see each other's faces.

"Wait, I know," he says quickly. "You were mad."

"Yeah, I was," I reply, trying to keep my jaw unclenched. "Why didn't you pick up or call ME back the first five times I called you?"

"I didn't want to talk to you until I got here 'cus I knew you'd talk me out of it," he responds a little sheepishly. "Thankfully, I remembered seeing the name of the hospital on a note you had back at the house. Good ol' Google took care of the rest."

Recovering, I turn back to my friends with the intention of making the introductions, but Rodney beats me to it.

"Maurice," says Maurice as the two shake hands.

"Marcus. And you are Rodney," Marcus smirks, extending his hand.

"That's me," Rodney smiles just before turning back to me.

"You know what," I say, turning to M & M, "go on up."

"Hold up," says Rodney. "You haven't even gone up to see him yet."

"It can wait," I reply, eyeing Rodney's rental car keys hanging out of his pocket.

"I'll catch up with you two later," I explain as I hand Marcus my car keys.

"Cool," replies Maurice.

"So am I in trouble?" Rodney asks as we approach the car.

"In trouble?" I reply, a little puzzled.

"I know you didn't want me to come with you."

He opens the car door for me. I don't think I'll ever get used to stuff like that. Maybe it's all the testosterone. Standing on my tippy toes, I kiss him on the cheek. Something I never thought I'd do in public, years or even just months ago.

"Baby, I never want to be away from you," I answer, burying my face in his chest. "This is just something that I thought I was supposed to do alone. I'm starting to think that I was very wrong."

"Whoa," replies Rodney, putting the back of his hand to my forehead. "Are you feeling all right?"

"Shut up!" I slap his hand away as I climb into the car.

"I'll be sure to remember that statement. I doubt I'll ever hear that again."

Just as I open my mouth to spew venom, he closes my door.

"Got you!" he shouts from the safety of the outside.

He laughs and points at me while running around to the driver's side of the car. He's definitely learning me. Considering that and how cute he can be, I guess I have to keep him around a little while longer.

Abomination

A couple of hours later, inside the Nordstrom's fitting room with Rodney . . .

"I'm too sexy for these pants, too sexy for these pants," he hums over his shoulder to me. "I know this is getting you hot." He laughs while stripping down to his black boxer briefs, revealing a muscular frame that never ceases to amaze and excite me.

He does look tastier than a Harold's Chicken Wing, but rather than feed his ego, I just smirk in response as he tries on the fifth suit.

"Baby, I told you that it ain't that deep." I sigh. "I don't even have to wear the suit I brought."

"Damn that," he replies, pulling up the slacks. "We going to yo church and then dinner with the fam. I ain't trying to look like a fool."

"You just like any excuse to shop," I laugh, throwing a shirt at him.

"Baby, this is like the NBA draft. I got to be G'd up."

He scrutinizes himself in the mirror.

"Damn!"

"What now, prima donna?" I groan from behind my clasped hands.

I tend to forget that for all Rodney's manly qualities, he can be just as bad as the most indecisive chick in the mall.

"That first blue shirt and tie combo will go better with this suit," he says.

I fight the urge to remind him how I had just said that almost forty-five minutes ago.

"Hold up," Rodney says, leaning down to kiss me on the cheek. "I'll be right back."

He runs out of the dressing room.

"Church," I sigh to myself.

I was late even for CPT (colored people time). Service was in full swing, complete with the high that only the Holy Spirit of God can bring. Thankfully, the majority of the medium-sized three-hundred-plus-people congregation was too preoccupied to take notice of my less-than-inconspicuous entrance. As usual, I waved, hugged, or kissed en route to my designated seat on the second of the thirty-plus pews. Of course, this was not a spot I'd pick for myself, but choir members who missed the processional were required to sit up front on the right until our part in the service. Even if I wasn't planning to sing, all men were encouraged to sit up front on the left. Many Sundays, I'd go toe to toe with the white-haired ushers or the balding deacons and hide out in the back with the rest of the heathen, but I just didn't have the resolve that morning.

While the service, in my opinion, was being carried out in the Spirit that God intended, it was still such a routine production. Before I knew it, it was time for me to take my place on the first row with the other "height disadvantaged" as the choir got situated. Sentenced to the spotlight yet again. We did two selections—the slow yet powerful "Order My Steps" and the crowd favorite "Make Me Better." As to be expected, they generated the spiritual and/or emotional responses the composers intended. Pastor encouraged the congregation, as a whole, to lift our voices in praise before thanking the Lord for another expression of HIS love and taking his text.

This morning, Pastor called our attention to several biblical passages, as opposed to just one, all lending evidence of the omnipotence of God. Through the scriptures, he reminded us over and over of how God could do anything. He called upon the congregation to bear witness, which the majority did in a resounding "amen"! We were reminded that God was able to create and maintain all of Creation.

"Amen!"

We were reminded that Christ was able to coexist as the Son of God and the Son of Man.

"Amen!"

How Christ walked the earth, lived, died, rose again, and secured blissful eternal salvation for all who call upon his name.

"Amen!"

The scriptures went on to say how the Holy Spirit of God imparted Himself in every true believer, enabling him (or her) to walk upright.

"Amen!"

How that same Spirit would help the liar to stop lying.

"Amen!"

Help the cheater to stop cheating.

"Amen!"

The fornicator to stop having premarital sex.

"Amen!"

The drunk to stop drinking.

"Amen!"

The dope dealer to stop dealing.

"Amen!"

The homosexual from being perverse in God's eyes.

"Amen!"

And of course, this was where the sermon took the turn I so desperately hoped and prayed to avoid every Sunday morning, evening, or otherwise.

"How can a man, made in God's own image, given more reason and logic than the animals, choose to lie with another man?" Pastor demanded.

Collective groans, moans, and general sounds of disgust filled the air, suffocating me.

"IT . . . IS . . . AN . . . ABOMINATION!"

"AMEN!"

A bit of my soul was shredded every time I heard these words. Because I usually sat directly behind or beneath Pastor, in view of the entire congregation, I just absorbed the blows, not wanting to betray myself to people who were, most likely, already suspicious as I had done countless Sundays before. As I had an infinite number of times before, I attempted, in vain, to count how many years, prayers, tears I had waited, prayed, shed, pleading with this same Almighty God to change me into something worthy of His love. Something worthy to be loved by these saints. Something worthy of loving myself. And it had never come. Once again, love appeared unobtainable. I decided that if I couldn't have it, then I didn't need or want it. I brought up my ageless defenses again. When service ended, I went through the usual motions—hugging, shaking hands, making my way to the door as quickly and as inconspicuously as possible.

Rather than running straight home to strip out of my good straight church boy attire, I drove around the city, trying to outrun the depression bombarding my entire being. Afraid of the formulation of yet another dark and destructive plot against myself. The mental and emotional defenses I had relied on for so long had eroded to a paper-thin veneer. In my mind's eye, I made out the tiniest light of sanity. In that moment of clarity, I prayed to God for the soundness of my mind. The Holy Spirit brought to my remembrance the multitude of blessings God had given me. I took that as my cue to thank God for everything I could consciously remember.

I thanked him for being who He is. I thanked him for Jesus. I thanked him for eternal salvation. I thanked him for the Holy Spirit's comforting presence. I thanked him for my life, my health, and my strength. I thanked him for a loving family and friends. I thanked him for food to eat. A place to sleep. Clothes to wear. For the necessities of life. For them in abundance. I thanked him for faith, hope, and love even though I thought they had yet to manifest. For the trials he had already brought me through. For those to come and the strength they would bring. I thanked him for victories and the resolution to my current troubles that no man could hope to fathom. With my mind a bit clearer, I pulled out my cell phone and took the first of many steps toward taking my happiness into my own hands.

"Calvin . . . can I please come over so that we can talk?"

* * *

From that afternoon on, things got so good between Calvin and me. It was beyond anything my mind could have ever conceived. We were damn near inseparable, sleeping together every night possible. Granted, sex was a huge motivator, but there was definitely an infatuation there as well. It was so evident in the way he catered to me, and he anticipated nearly all my wants and needs. The opening of doors, cooking all my meals. The way I'd catch him just staring at me only to answer "you" when I'd ask what he was looking at. Every moment a sensation of infinity. The unexplainable feeling that you have always been and will always be encompassed by love. The typical beginning of a courtship. It was all I could do to match gesture for gesture all up until he offered me his key only three weeks into our exclusive status. Looking back, that definitely marked the turning point. Hindsight after all is 20/20 as someone once said.

Serious Conversations

That evening, my cell phone wakes me to the comfort of a king-sized bed I share with Rodney. For a split second, I forget that we are in the suite at Oak Brook Marriot that Rodney had checked into prior to tracking me down at the hospital. The phone rings again. I wrestle free of Rodney's arms and legs to answer. Not the norm for anyone that knows me, but the ring has a special tone. I smile at the site of the caller ID.

"Wassup, Eric?"

I smile through the phone.

"Wassup, big bro?"

It is always so crazy to hear my 250 lb. solid, 6'6" younger brother refer to me as *big*, but as usual, I go with it.

"Nothing much. Just running the streets like I never moved away," I answer while situating myself at the foot of the bed. "How you been?"

"Everything is all right with me."

"I was still hoping to see your new place before I fly back out."

"You not missing anything," he responds. "Don't get me wrong. I'm cool with it, but that's because of all the work I plan to put into it."

"Yeah, I know," I chuckle along with memory for the first time this weekend, thinking back to my first studio apartment. "It takes time, but in the end, you'll look back on it as the best thing you've ever done."

"Yeah, I know," Eric replies. "I called the house, and Mom said that you'd been gone since yesterday. You catch up with your friends still living here in the city."

"Yeah," I smirk while nudging Rodney who's starting to snore pretty loud. "Plus a few flew in town this weekend too."

Rodney rolls over on cue, falling silent.

"Cool, cool. So you leave anyone special back in Vegas?"

For the second time this weekend, I'm knocked off balance. My brother knows I'm gay, but aside from some of our shared biblical upbringing, I don't know how he feels. I know he loves me and hasn't changed toward me. Perhaps that's all I need to know.

"Well," I begin sheepishly, "I left him in Vegas, but he sort of followed me."

"Are you serious?" he asks.

After the longest second of silence, he finally laughs, and I breathe again.

"Man, that is cool," he says in between laughing. "Ya'll must be really serious."

"Yeah, but . . .," I sigh.

"Hey, I ain't telling Mom and Dad nothing." I mentally picture him holding his hands up, indicating *I'm not getting into that*. "That is for you to tell, but I will say that if you're happy, I'm happy for you. I know we don't talk about this stuff much, but in light of what little I know that you've been through all these years, I'd rather know that you are happy."

My throat threatens to close up.

"Eric, thank you," I finally manage. "I didn't think that I could be happier than I was before hearing that."

"Well, you should know that Regina feels the same way. I didn't tell her, but she did put it together."

"Well, she did grow up in the age of *Will and Grace*," I think out loud.

We talk for a few more minutes, ending the conversation in anticipation of seeing each other tomorrow at dinner. I lay there awhile longer, listening to Rodney's heavy breathing, and decide to make my way into the shower before anyone sends out the hounds in search of me. Walking toward the bathroom, I step on something sharp.

"Ouch!" I shout, one part surprise, two parts anger.

"You all right, baby?" Rodney grumbles, still half-asleep.

"Yeah," I reply despite a tight jaw. "I just stepped on your keys!"

I hobble the rest of the way to the shower and turn on the water. The steam fills the room while I brush my teeth and watch my reflection in the vanity fade away.

"Hmmm," I groan, finally stepping into the inch or so of hot water, stinging the new scratch in the sole of my foot. "What is so hard about putting away your keys?" I think aloud.

I release the petty tension with a sigh.

* * *

In all fairness, it wasn't the exchange of keys that brought on the storm but the clouds, in retrospect, definitely began to gather in the distance. For a while, I prided myself on having not accepted his key for a **whole** *week and* **several** *discussions later. Even patted myself on the back for not giving up* **my** *key until* **two** *weeks later, but just like the Bible says, pride comes before a great fall. I'm sure that's in Proverbs somewhere. It sounds wise. Anyway, it was around that time that we began to have a number of serious conversations. Some far too early. His insistence on moving in together. A lot of nagging and unrealistic demands on my part. And at least one conversation far too late.*

"I think it would be a good idea if we got tested together," Calvin suggested as we sat in the tub together after one of our steamy afternoon lovemaking sessions.

"That is a very good idea," I replied as he washed my back.

We were both **certain** *of our status but finally decided that, as a couple, we should* **know** *what we, as friends, had always told each other. Given his known past with a number of serious drugs and having sex under the influence (to this day, not sure if condoms were always used or not) and my own partner a month for the four months prior to our first night (even with protection), we were definitely kids playing with a loaded gun.*

Due to some differences in our insurance, me Blue Cross/Blue Shield PPO and him N/A, we went separate ways in regard to getting our tests done with the agreement that we'd share the printed results. In our minds, it was all a formality in light of at least one prior year of negative status apiece. This was also despite several unprotected encounters together. Careless. Naïve. Ignorant. Arrogant. Stupid. Even years later, no word appears adequate.

"Baby," calls Rodney from across my steamy tropical scene. "Yo boy Marcus on the phone."

The hounds have been released.

"He say he thought you might want to get yo clothes and yo rental back when we came up for air."

Status Update

After stopping by Mom's to check in and get my Sunday best, Rodney and I make our way down to the W. I was somewhat surprised that he didn't insist on coming into Mom's house. Maybe he's not as eager about tomorrow as he appeared.

"Just in time for a cocktail, I see," I say, walking into M & M's suite with Rodney.

"Yeah," says Maurice in the mirror, trying on a fresh white-on-white White Sox cap. "We just got through pulling ourselves together."

"My, my," chuckles Marcus from the bar, spying Rodney and I holding hands. "Guess you not mad at him anymore, hun."

"I'll have a vodka and cranberry," I respond.

"You know the rule. Your first visit **might** get you service. From there, you are on your own," Marcus replies, walking to his seat. "By the way, cute attempt at changing the subject. Cute, but hardly effective."

I look up into Rodney's grinning face.

"What?"

"I'll have a beer," he smirks while raising his hands defensively. "Thanks, Benson."

He quickly backs away toward the couch to join M & M also laughing at me.

After an hour or so of drinks and sports highlights . . .

"You guys mind if I use the bathroom?" asks Rodney, already on his feet.

"No prob," Maurice answers.

Just as the door closes . . .

"This is the last thing I have to say on this," Maurice begins, eyeing me very deliberately. "You should go see him."

I move to look toward the restroom.

"You know who I mean," he continues. "It really isn't what you think it is . . ."

The restroom door opens again.

"Well, gentlemen," sighs Marcus, "I believe it is about that time. Otherwise, I'll be knocked out."

*　*　*

We trail each other to the Generator, another club in the Warehouse District that we used to frequent back in our day.

"I've got it, boys," says Rodney as he pays all our way into the club and then holds the door for us all.

"Thanks," Maurice replies.

Aside from the different address and a bit more square footage, the club is practically the same as the night before. The latest hip-hop, rap, and other popular urban dance music playing loudly, smoky air, flashing lights, and literally damned near the exact same overcrowded clientele.

"This is a pretty jumping spot," says Rodney over the sound of Amerie's "This One Thing." "I'm off to the bar. You boys what anything? It's on me."

"I'll have a Budweiser," Marcus answers.

"Same here," says Maurice.

"I think I've had enough alcohol for the night," I shout over the music.

"I'll get you a bottle of water, then," Rodney suggests.

He stoops down to plant a kiss on my cheek and makes his way to the bar, just visible across the crowded, active dance floor. I was a little surprised that he didn't insist on me coming with him. Rodney is on his best behavior, taking a break from his normal role as alpha male. As the night goes on, I notice painfully obvious attempts at not hovering around me or staring down everything that makes the slightest bit of eye contact with me. Definitely his best behavior.

He and I have had a good run this past year and a half. According to my calculations, that translates into seven years of marriage in terms of a gay relationship. Of course, there were some bumps in the road and, sometimes, when both of us just wanted to quit, but our good days far outweigh our bad ones. He is the first person I've been compelled to be completely open with. It always amazes me when a person can know the deepest, darkest things about you and not run away screaming in terror.

"Are you sure you can deal with me and all . . . my baggage?" I once asked Rodney while we sat under a desert night sky full of stars, on the cool hood of his Camry.

He slightly tightened his arms, which encircled me from behind.

"My biggest bets have always paid off the most," he said. "I don't see why this would be any different."

Not since Calvin had it even occurred to me to consider a life with someone else by my side. There were only a few years between closing my heart behind Calvin and Rodney's appearance like a thief in the night. Looking back, it seemed more like an eternity. The front I presented to the world shouted "Leave Me the Fuck Alone," all the while, deep down inside, it was the last thing I needed. I got so good at baring the world outside that I failed to notice that I had imprisoned myself. I still wonder how Rodney had managed to get in.

Physically, Rodney is a dream come true, but in our short time together, he definitely has proven himself to be so much more than a handsome face and perfectly sculpted body. There is the confident way he carries himself, his ambitious, open, friendly nature, and of course, his devotion to us. He's not just someone I could live with but also someone I didn't want to live without. The more I turn it all over in my mind, the more similar he and the Calvin of long ago seem. It unsettles me just a bit. At that moment, Rodney slips his arms around my waist from behind.

He lowers his lips to my ear and whispers, "You thinking pretty hard over here. You okay?"

Rather than part my lips to lie, I just nod in the affirmative. So much for being completely open. Jennifer Lopez's "Get Right" comes on. From the corner of my eye, I see M & M each partnered up and dancing like no one's watching.

"Let's show everyone your moves, Mr. Black Satin," I shout while pulling him onto the dance floor.

Within a few minutes, we hear Kenya Gruv's "Top of the World," and everyone slows to a grind. As Rodney and I slow-dance, I attempt to be optimistic. I choose to see the similarities of my past and present more as a promise of good to come rather than a precursor of doom.

* * *

At the end of the predetermined week of waiting, Calvin explained to me that the results he went in for had been delayed due to some error on the lab's part.

"They said to come back on Monday," *he told me one Thursday evening.*

Early the following Monday afternoon, we decided to have lunch by the lake while waiting for his appointment. Living and loving each other under the bluest of skies. That was the only part of that blissful weekend I can allow myself to recall. On the trip from the clinic back to his place, he assured me that everything checked out fine, but he wanted to show me the printed results when we got home. There he tells me how the doctor told him on the previous Thursday there was a chance that he might have syphilis again. Again?

"I contracted syphilis about eight or ten years ago, but I got treatment for it," *he said in a matter-of-fact manner.* "I was pretty sure that the antibodies were what came up on the test. The doctor said that we shouldn't have any sexual contact until he got in touch with the health center that treated me back in the day. He didn't reach them as of today but was certain that I was okay. He suggested that we both get treatments just as a precaution."

Maybe it was the weariness from the day. Maybe it was the way he looked at me as he explained all this so calmly. Maybe it was the paperwork indicating that he appeared clean. Whatever the cause, I listened, responded absently, and took a nap. But when I awoke, so did my common sense with a smoldering calmness.

"So the doctor told you days ago, on Thursday, that we shouldn't have sex," *I began, each comment more of a statement than a question.*

"Yes, but I knew you were coming over this weekend and . . ."

"But you thought that you were okay," *I continued, ignoring his last comment for the moment.*

"Yes . . ."

"And you kept this information to yourself, and we had sex anyway."

He just stared at me.

"You do realize that you took a very serious decision that affected me completely out of my hands."

His gaze dropped to his hands that unconsciously fumbled with the comforter.

"So in the end, it was all about you?"

Appalled at the thought of touching him, I lowered my head until I matched his line of sight. We both returned to an upright position.

"I would be lying if I said that I wasn't disappointed, to say the least," I said, visibly attempting to keep my voice in check. "It is hard for me to know that a person who I love and trust would be this . . ."

I attempted to swallow a few sobs, some venomous language, and a few very negative emotions. I just looked at him for a second.

"You know what, whatever, I forgive you, okay?" I said in a hushed, hurried tone. "I will do my best to just put this out of my mind."

That is what my mouth said, but my heart wasn't so sure of when that would actually happen. We slept on separate sides of the bed that night.

Calvin and I woke with very little conversation that next morning before I set out for my own test results. The weight of the next hour shifted the scales with such titanic force that they nearly shattered.

* * *

The music stops, and the club lights come up.

"What the hell?" I think out loud. "What happened to last call?"

"That was somewhere between the time you were brooding and when you were sulking," says Marcus, walking up from behind.

"Well, add this frown to that list."

"Breakfast, anyone?" asks Maurice.

I looked down to my watch.

It was 4:30 a.m.!

"Naw," I answer, looking at Rodney. "If we go straight to bed, we can still get in a good three hours of sleep."

"Hmm," smacks Maurice. "You run back to the hotel, get your box banged out real good, and pop up in time to praise the Lord."

"Yeah, just like a heathen," I laugh. "Here."

I toss my rental car keys with a smirk.

"See you guys at dinner tomorrow, right?"

"Yeah," Maurice answers.

"Not going to miss a chance to finally meet the family," laughs Marcus as we file out of the club.

Leviathan

Turmoil
hideousness unleashed
emerging with a splash

Gaining height
recoiling, coiling, recoiling
eclipsing the dawn
ancient monarch of the air
traversing sea and sky

Diving, plummeting with
ravenous intent
appetite insatiable
gargantuan talons, looming,
ominous tools of torture
nearing unsuspecting prey

7/10/00

Seron Wright Jr.

SUNDAY

A Bit More Slack

Those three hours of sleep are more like three minutes. From what Rodney tells me the next morning, I spent the majority of that time wrestling in my sleep.

"I had to hold you so you would stop hitting me," he calls, somewhat agitated from the bathroom. "What were you dreaming about?"

"I don't really remember."

The second lie in only just five or so hours. Well, it was a half-truth but still not a good trend. While he showers, I lie back and close my eyes, vaguely recalling the sensation of feeling bound.

Chains . . . bound by chains? Yes, bound in chains. For some reason, I'm certain that I had been bound for a very long time. I recall being too tired to struggle anymore. No. Not tired, at least not physically. The emotional fatigue of one who finally gives up.

"Loose him and let him go," commands a voice that comes from nowhere and everywhere at the same time.

Immediately, the chains spring open.

"Arise and walk," the voice calls.

I stand and move to obey but find that something has my right hand. Looking down, I see that I have a firm hold on one of the chains. For some reason, I keep pulling at it in vain rather than letting it go.

"It's your turn," Rodney whispers in my ear, waking me for a second time.

I stumble into the bathroom, sleepy and confused.

Arriving late to church, I realize that I had let my pessimism and self-involvement get the better of me once again. There's hardly any opportunity for anything I'd most likely have grossly misinterpreted as an *interrogation* from the familiar faces of the congregation upon my entry with Rodney's unfamiliar face. Rodney cleans up pretty good in his brand-new black pin-striped Sean John suit, crisp medium-starched white shirt, and a daring pink tie all complete with fresh shiny Aldo slip-ons.

"Good morning," I say to a number of familiar faces as we make our way to the sanctuary.

"This way, please," instructs one of the ushers greeting us at the door.

Following my lead, he and I are obedient and follow the usher who seats us right up front. Of course, that draws much unwanted attention to the both of us. I spot my parents and some other family members mixed throughout the congregation. Numerous longing stares from the women in Rodney's direction nearly cause me to burst into fits of laughter. That, of course, is when I am not preoccupied with other looks that just seem a bit too inquisitive for my comfort level. I face forward and focus on the remainder of the service. The choir favors us with two selections, "Order My Steps" and "Make Me Better."

"Man, this choir really has the place rocking," Rodney says to me over the sounds of the organ and the drums with a smile.

"Glad you are enjoying yourself," I reply, relaxing more into my seat.

Finally, Pastor takes his place behind the pulpit, beginning the morning sermon. Surprisingly, he reads from Exodus, recounting how God delivered the Hebrews from the sorrows of Egyptian slavery. All the usual elements of the story are there—Pharaoh's initial refusal to free the slaves, the ten plagues, the parting of the Red Sea, the complaints of the Hebrews as they wandered the desert and how some of them thought they would have been better off back in Egypt. As a result, a number of them weren't permitted to see the same Promised Land for which they had originally fled from Egypt.

He briefly touches on how God gave them the Ten Commandments and the hundreds of laws that were later made as a result, all providing a temporary standard by which the Hebrews were to live.

Pastor then goes to the New Testament, pointing out several passages in which Peter, Paul, and other apostles of Christ reminded the newly converted Christian Jews and Gentiles of how Jesus's sacrifice on the cross fulfilled all those laws. By following his example of self-sacrificing, love freed them from the impossible burden of attempting to observe all those laws, and how love encompassed them all. Many, however, still preferred the ancient laws to Christ's new commandment, heaping unnecessary burden upon themselves and one another. Just as I begin to feel the consequences of my nocturnal activity, Pastor drives the point home.

"God, in the form of Christ, freed us of our sorrows and burdens. He desires for us to walk in that freedom, but some of us are still bound. Why? What chains can bind us when the Lord Himself has set us free? Some of us would, no doubt, answer that we are still bound by past situations and old sorrows. But the same God who declared the Hebrews free, the same Christ who freed the newly founded church in the scriptures has declared that you too are free. So I ask again, why are you still bound? Why aren't you walking in the freedom that Christ has granted you? Could it be that you refuse to let go of the things, the situations, the people that bind you? Are you clinging to tradition, to religion while forsaking faith and spirituality? Could it be that you are stopping yourself from walking in freedom?"

Immediately, I feel something mentally loosen. Not totally, but there is definitely a bit more *slack*.

After shaking the hand of Pastor, the associate ministers, one of which is my stepfather, and the deacons, I lead Rodney across the church in search of my mother. As usual, I reach my father's mother, my stepmother, and my father first. Along the way, I exchange hugs, kisses, and handshakes with countless familiar, welcoming faces.

"Rodney. Nice to meet you," Rodney repeats over and over to those we encounter, ever the warm, outgoing type.

How did he end up with me again? At long last, I reach my mother's side just as a number of her visiting relatives walk up.

"What happened to you this morning, sugar?" asks my maternal grandmother, Alease, as we hug.

"Lost the fight with my sheets," I reply, taking in her warmth.

I introduce Rodney to the family, intermittingly greeting other church members as they go by.

"Well, let's get a move on," says my stepfather, having finished his duties in the ministers' receiving line.

"We do still need to stop at the store and pick up a few things on the way home," Mom adds.

Everyone breaks for their vehicles.

"That was pretty cool," says Rodney, breaking the silence on the way back to Mom's house. "I haven't been to church since . . . hmmm . . . maybe I shouldn't finish that."

"Yeah, it was a good service," I respond, laughing a little. "That is, of course, when I was focused on it."

"You mean instead of all the people?" he suggests, sparing a glance away from the road over to me.

"Yeah," I reply.

"Could you blame them?"

He takes one of his hands from the steering wheel and rests it on top of mine.

"Baby, they haven't seen you in years and then you come back looking GOOD," he says with a suspicious grin. "Not to mention . . ."

"I got Mr. Black Satin as my man," I insert, beating him to the punch line.

"And you know it."

He leans over to plant a kiss on my cheek.

"Make a right up here," I point. "You do look pretty good in a suit."

I take his hand in mine.

A few more turns and compliments bring us to our destination.

"So you want me to come up with you?" Rodney asks as we sit in the hospital parking lot.

"Naw," I reply absently.

I turn to focus on him.

"But thanks. I won't be long."

"Take your time. I'll be right here."

Past Meets Present

Bits and pieces of memory, fractured by my past abuse of a few too many sleeping pills, struggle to surface as I make my way through the hospital hallways. It amazes me that there are so many gay people in the world today. So many of us just barely escaped the most earnest attempts at suicide, not to mention other self-destructive behavior all stemming from self-loathing and a need to cope. I cast away the remembrance of my own brief stay here and force myself across the final threshold. I find him in a restful sleep. Though his face is unshaven and not quite as full, every part of me recognizes him immediately. Not intending to stay long, I move to the foot of Calvin's hospital bed.

"I just . . . can't do this anymore," I hear Calvin say to me with eyes that mourn far too early.

"We ran the test twice," Dr. Hanson said with eyes that attempted to soften the blow. "They indicate that you are HIV positive."

"Okay," I heard myself say with an eerie calm.

"Does this news surprise you?"

"Yes."

My voice threatened to crack. There was more conversation about my emotional welfare, in light of my past experiences with depression. Together, we deduced that I was infected over a year ago, the same time at which I was diagnosed with what we could only conclude was a sinus infection. I left his office armed with the number to a disease specialist and a resolve not to have my life interrupted by this new information. I called everyone I had the slightest sexual contact with since the time of my last negative test while attempting to complete the other errands I had previously scheduled for the day. For some reason, I couldn't get anything accomplished. The store didn't have the part I needed. The mechanic couldn't take anyone else for the day. And so on . . .

"I think you should come home," Calvin suggested while I drove around aimlessly.

"And so now I need to schedule an appointment with another doctor to learn my T-cell count and viral load," I explained to Calvin back at his place. "I need to figure out if I need to start medications and—"

"Stop," Calvin interrupted.

"But I need to—"

He wrapped his arms around me. The dam cracked and the first tear flowed. I was unaware at the time, but the same stream would run off and on for months to come.

I felt myself sinking. I pushed away from Calvin's chest and took his hands. I looked within and reached out for the only help I had ever really known.

"Father, God," I began, "I come acknowledging you as the Almighty, the only wise, the only living God. The Maker, the Creator, and Sustainer of all of creation . . . I come to you"—holding back sobs—"acknowledging you as Christ, the King of kings, Lord of lords, the one who died and rose again for my sake . . . I come acknowledging you as the Holy Spirit of God, the one who leads us, guides us, and comforts us. The one who seals us until the day of redemption . . . the Alpha and Omega. The Beginning and the End. All that I could ever need . . . I come acknowledging you as all these things . . . I come asking you for forgiveness for my sins. For sins of commission, those things I've done that you said not to do. For sins of omission, those things you said to do that I left undone. For sins of permission, those things against your will that I allowed to be done . . . I come thanking you and praising your name. I thank you for who you are and for all that you have done and for all that you will do. I thank you for the good and the bad . . . I praise you. I magnify you. I say hallelujah to your name. I thank you for the gift of your name, the power in your name, the wisdom, and the ability to call on your name . . . Father, I come to you because . . . because I don't know what to do . . . I don't . . . know . . . what to do . . ."

The dam finally gave way, along with every emotional and mental defense. My prayers bypassed my mouth and flew from my heart right up to heaven. I cried until my head ached. I sobbed until I couldn't breathe. My body trembled until I was exhausted from the tension in my muscles. I prayed for myself, all those infected and affected. I prayed for peace, for understanding, for strength, for courage, for the times when I wouldn't have the will to pray.

"Are you okay?" I asked Calvin, finally composing myself nearly a half an hour later.

"I'm okay," he replied, looking on with concern.

"Are you worried?" I asked.

"I'm fine," he said, pulling me back into his arms. "Lay down."

We lay down on the bed. I eventually fell asleep.

"I need to run out for a minute," Calvin said, waking me later that evening.

"Okay," I mumbled before drifting back to sleep.

I rolled over at 2:00 a.m. and found that he hadn't come home yet. I awoke sometime that night to the sound of Calvin saying his nightly prayers, his voice just barely audible. I heard light sobbing. He climbed into bed and pulled me close.

"Are you sure you're okay?" I asked in a hoarse whisper.

"Yeah, I'm fine," he answered while kissing me on the cheek.

That first week was a mixture of confused emotions, sick days, doctor's appointments, and information gathering. I steamed ahead on the "Proactive Train" destination, some sense of normality, with Calvin acting as coengineer when I allowed him to do so. The next month brought support groups, drug regimens, the anticipation of talking with my family and friends, and most importantly, questions from Calvin. Actually, it was the same question rephrased over and over and over.

"Did you know your status when we started seeing each other?"

I repeatedly answered, "No, I didn't," with the patience of Job, which I never would have guessed that I could have possessed.

On some level, I knew that the repeated inquiry was borne out of concern for me as well as fear for his own well-being. Days turned into weeks. Weeks became months. We saw each other less and less. We talked less and less. The time apart was a mixed blessing. Daily, I struggled to build a new resolve, to construct a new fortitude. One day, the flood of tears began to recede. Finally, out of anguish and frustration, I cornered Calvin at home.

"I've talked with some of my friends," I explained, sitting on the opposite end of his couch.

"That's really good," he replied while staring at the TV.

"And I'm finally getting used to the meds."

He pointed the remote at the TV and continued to channel surf.

I slid over to sit closer to him, crossing the gap that our mutual fears had created.

"How about you?"

"What?" he asked, rubbing his hand along his trembling leg.

"I asked how you are doing."

"Oh. I'm cool . . . You know . . ."

"Can you please look at me?" I asked, reaching for his hand out of pure instinct.

He casually moved it to rub his head, obviously avoiding my touch.

"You know I have to leave out in a minute," he began after a moment pregnant with silence.

"Calvin, we really need to talk. It's been three months."

"I can't right now," he said, still refusing to look my way.

I looked at him, trying in vain to will him to face me, but he wouldn't.

"Okay," I sighed. "I'm going to leave, then."

I stood and turned to go. I heard the remote fall to the couch. He quickly, desperately grabbed my arm. I heard his ragged breathing before I looked back down to him. Calvin looked up at me, his eyes pleading for understanding, for forgiveness.

"I just . . . can't do this anymore."

I was surprised to hear his voice crack over the sound of my own heart breaking. The sensation of infinity that we had always shared finally collapsed as our hands let go. I turned away for what I believed to be forever that day and closed the door behind me.

EPITOME

"Excuse me," says a man entering Calvin's hospital room. "I hope I'm not interrupting, but you must be Seron."

The shock of my abrupt return to the present is nothing compared to the appearance of the stranger before me.

"I'm Sean," says a man who is damned near my mirror image.

To be more accurate, he is more of what I used to look like. We share the same approximate short thin build, a similar medium-brown complexion. The most visible difference is that he wears the shoulder-length sandy brown dreads I had forsaken a few years back. Painfully, I even admit to myself that he is most likely a few years younger as well.

"We spoke on the phone," Sean explains, extending his hand to me.

"Yes," I reply, gathering myself. "I remember."

We shake hands.

"Well, he wasn't kidding about you and I being alike," Sean adds. "As far as appearance goes."

"It is a little unsettling, to say the least."

He swallows hard, apparently not prepared for my blunt manner.

"The chemo wipes him out," he says, turning to look at Calvin. "They also gave him something to help him sleep awhile ago."

Chemo?

"Who would have guessed that a man who guards his health so closely, dieting, exercising, abstaining from drugs, and everything else would have to deal with lung cancer from secondhand smoke."

Sean walks over and kneels by Calvin's sleeping side. He takes one of Calvin's hands into the two of his. Behind my stone face, my mind is working a mile a minute. *Chemo? Lung cancer? So he doesn't have . . . I didn't give him . . .*

I recall what Maurice said last night.

"It really isn't what you think it is."

Oh my god!

"Hell, he was even so damned adamant about wearing our seat belts just to go around the corner," Sean continues. "But I'm sure he was like that with you too."

"He apparently learned a lot," I answer in the midst of my clouded comprehension.

I walk over to Calvin's other side, staring down at the sleeping stranger. Time has altered more than his appearance. I kneel down and take his other hand, surprising myself, not to mention making Sean somewhat uncomfortable. If he were a cat, his back would be arched and each hair standing on end. I bring my head down, not wanting to move Calvin's hand too much more, and I pray silently.

"You okay, Lil' Magic?"

I look back up at Calvin's sleeping form.

"Is something wrong?" asks Sean.

I look across to him.

"Did he . . ." I begin.

Sean's look of confusion matches my own imagined facial expression.

"No . . . Never mind."

I move to his face and hear Sean's breathing stop. I lightly kiss Calvin on the forehead.

"He should wake up in a little bit," Sean says, regaining his composure as I begin to stand up.

"That's good," I answer while readjusting my clothes.

I reach across Calvin's chest and shake Sean's hand.

"It was nice to meet you," he says.

"It was nice of you to say so," I reply. "Thank you for calling me . . . and all his friends."

I look back down at Calvin for a second more and leave, closing the door behind me.

Dreams Do Come True

"I want a divorce!" Yasmine shouts to me, running across the yard.

Mom's small family dinner has exploded to at least thirty-some odd guests. At the last minute, she had changed plans to have a backyard BBQ instead. A pretty good idea considering the warm weather.

"What!" I exclaim.

"Well, I can't exactly run away with Rodney if I'm still married to you."

I look past her to Rodney, who is hemmed in by Jordan, Donna, and Shawn, looking over to me for a rescue.

I laugh, finally understanding the joke and seeing him in peril.

"Don't worry," she continues. "I won't fight you for the house and kids. I don't want a lengthy court battle."

"'Ron,'" calls Eric. "The guys are here."

"I'll have my lawyer call you in the morning," Yasmine chuckles with a wave and a wink before running back over to Rodney's new fan club.

"Guess who just flew in this morning," says Maurice.

He and Marcus part.

"Hey, cutie," Rich says, emerging from behind them with a smile.

"Mr. Richie," I cry out with surprise while running over to hug him. "What are you doing back in the continental United States?"

"Well, M & M finally caught up with me via e-mail and told me about our little reunion—" he began.

"Not an easy task," Marcus interrupts, "when dealing with a transient soul such as this."

"Whatever," Rich retorts. "So like I was saying before I was so rudely interrupted. I got the e-mail and hopped the first plane from the Dominican Republic."

"Well, I'm so glad you did," I say as we finally separate from our friendly embrace.

"Now that you Judies have popped your bobby pins," laughs Maurice. "Where is the spread?"

"Forget the spread. Where is this man I've heard so much about?" Rich asks.

"The spread is beside the garage," I answer, looking toward M & M. "Help yourselves."

They walk off.

"And I'll introduce you," I say, turning to Rich.

"So the boys say that Calvin seems okay," Rich says as we walk across the yard.

"I think so," I answer. "As best as can be expected given the circumstances."

"Ah," he sighs. "So you did go see him."

"Yeah. The new boifriend may have exaggerated a bit."

"And you met the new boi?"

"I'll elaborate later," I explain as we reach Rodney and the girls.

"Rodney, ladies, this is Rich, another member of the circle," I say, interrupting what appears to be a good ol'-fashioned interrogation. "Rich, this is Shawn, Donna, Jordan, and Yasmine."

"Nice to meet you all," he says, extending his hand to each of them in turn.

"And this is . . ."

"Rodney," Rodney says, extending his hand and seizing on an opportunity to escape.

"Good job," Rich says, looking back over his shoulder to me with a wink.

"Um, can you show me to the bathroom?" Rodney asks, sounding like a helpless toddler.

I choose to exercise mercy at the expense of the pure comedy the situation affords me.

"Excuse us, girls," I say. "Rich, help yourself to the food."

Rodney releases a sigh.

"What?" I ask.

"Yo girlfriends are nice but, uh . . ." Rodney begins as we get out of earshot.

"But a bit vicious," I laugh, concluding the matter.

"Uh, yeah," he says, loosening his collar.

"And that is when they like you. So are you actually going to the bathroom?"

"I think I better," he says with a sigh. "I don't want to get in trouble with yo girls."

I lead him through the enclosed back porch to the guest restroom, right off the kitchen.

"Here you go," I say, gesturing through the open door. "I'll be checking on the folks in the living room just in case you need me."

"Cool. Thanks."

Family and friends of all ages and persuasions are all over the house. I have always anticipated mixing my different social circles, but as always, it works out better than I would have thought.

"You know, we have to get a game of spades going," says my cousin Neisha as I enter the dining room.

"He probably scared we gonna smoke him and whatever sorry partner he can find like last time," my cousin Esther teases.

"Things might be a lil' different with two Vegas transplants in the house this time," I respond. "Let me check on everything and get Rodney."

"We got winners," says Regina, indicating herself and Eric's girlfriend Trina.

"I hope spades is the only *habit* you've been working on in Sin City, nephew," calls my aunt Amina from the adjourning living room.

"You know my nephew don't part ways with his money all too quick," says my uncle Nathan sitting beside her.

"You got that right, Uncle," I respond, walking into the living room. "Mom, do you need anything? Anybody want something else from the kitchen?"

"No, I think we're all set," Mom answers.

"You guys can get another table and some chairs out of the garage and set it up in the yard to play on," says my stepfather.

"I'll get it," says Rodney who had just appeared over my shoulder.

"I'll help him," adds my sister Regina's *friend* Jonathan.

The next few hours are filled with laughter over old jokes and the fun of making new ones. Cards and dominoes making loud contact with tables and a lot of shit talking. The earsplitting shouts of "MICKEY MOUSE BUILT A HOUSE. HOW MANY BRICKS DID HE USE?" "NOT IT!" and "READY OR NOT HERE I COME" from the kids playing all around the outside of the house. The snoring of the older people inside who had overindulged in the barbequed ribs, chicken, and burgers, spaghetti, taco salad, and other fattening foods. As the daylight slowly disappeared, so did the food and the guests.

"Make sure you remember to call me when you land tomorrow," says my father as we hug before he leaves out of the door to follow his mother, my stepmother and my stepbrother and stepsisters.

"I'll call as soon as the plane touches down," I reply.

"It was so good to see you," says Donna, tears beginning to form in her eyes.

"Oh girl, don't start," laughs Jordan.

"Right," I add, "or we'll all be over here crying."

I hug them both at the same time.

"All right, move around," says Shawn, fighting her way into the embrace. "I'll expect my airline ticket in the mail. And I don't fly coach!"

"I'll work on that," I respond. "And while I'm at it, I'll make four reservations at the Grand Luxor."

"I'll let you hold on to my new husband for a lil' while longer in exchange for some of this action," says Yasmine, creating a space for herself within the huddle.

"I promise not to stay away for so long next time," I say to them all over our collective laughter and a few sobs.

"I'll drive M & M back to the hotel," Rich offers.

"Yeah, we're taking him out for the evening," Marcus adds.

"I'm thinking we need a full week next time we get together," says Maurice.

"Yeah, Labor Day is right around the corner," I agree. "But let's do NYC next time."

"Sounds like a plan to me," he replies.

"You sure you guys don't need help with the rest of this stuff?" asks Rodney as I walk him to his car.

"Well, the girls helped my sister and cousins in the kitchen," I respond. "You, Jonathan, and the guys helped straightened up the backyard. All I really have left to do is pack."

"Cool. So I guess I'll meet you at the airport in the morning then," he says, wrapping his arms around me.

"At 10:00 a.m. sharp. You sure you can make it through one more night without me?"

He responds with a long kiss. One of his hands drops to my butt and gives it a quick light pat.

"I guess so," he says in a dejected tone reminiscent of a child who is told he can't touch dessert until after eating all his vegetables.

"See you in the morning," I laugh.

He gives me another quick peck on the lips before getting into the car. I watch him drive off and walk back into the house. On my way into my bedroom, I see my mom in the kitchen, situating some of the leftovers in the refrigerator.

"Need any help?" I ask.

"Just finishing up," she answers.

"Thanks for everything," I say, sitting down at the table. "I hope it wasn't too overwhelming."

"Oh, it was no problem. With everyone helping out so much, I hardly had to lift a finger."

"Did Grandma and Amina call to say they all made it in safely?"

"Yeah, about twenty minutes ago. I think you and Rodney were outside at the time," she says, closing the refrigerator door.

She sits down across the table.

For a moment, the ceiling fan above us and the hum of the fridge are the only sounds in the room.

"He seems pretty nice."

"Yeah," I reply, looking down to my hands that are fumbling with my shirt. "He really is."

"So how is your health?"

"Well, my last checkup was about two months ago." I look back up to her. "My T-cells are up to 550, and my viral load is still undetectable."

"And how are things with the medications?"

"I'm down to just one pill a day with no serious side effects."

"Are you taking the vitamins I sent you?"

"Yes."

"That's good," she says with a sigh.

"You know that your fathers and I don't totally understand and accept all this," she begins after another uncomfortable pause.

This—summing up my lifestyle, my relationship with Rodney.

"I know," I say barely above a whisper.

"Oh, before I forgot," she says before ducking into the dining room. "I thought you might want to take this back with you."

She returns to her seat and hands something across the table to me.

The small piece of poster board looks maybe a month or two old as opposed to the ten or fifteen years it had actually aged. Even the colors from the Crayola brand paint and gold glitter seem just as bright as the day the plaque was made.

"I can't believe that you kept this!" I exclaim in disbelief. "Where did you find it?"

"I can't even remember," she answers. "We were in your old room getting ready to remodel, and I just saw it. I knew I had to show it to you."

At first I could just barely remember creating the high school freshman art assignment.

"For your final assignment we are going to be combining the painting and calligraphy exercises we did last week," the teacher explained. *"I want you to create a plaque. Pick whatever design you want for the background and print your name and future occupation in calligraphy."*

One or two read lawyer.

Several read accountant.

Mine read . . .

Seron Wright Jr.
Author

Mom gets up from her seat and crosses over to me. She puts her arms around me and hugs me as tight as she can. Somehow managing to transfer something intangible through touch.

"You should know that we will always accept and love you," she says. "I'm so proud of who you are and what you have accomplished."

"Thank you."

She kisses me on the forehead before we separate.

"I think we should both call it a night," she suggests.

"You're right."

Following an age-old routine, I check the locks on the back and side doors and turn off the kitchen lights while she waits at the door to the dining room.

"Good night," she says, making her way upstairs to join my stepfather already fast asleep in their room.

"Good night," I reply, walking to my old room.

Godsend

An eternity of isolation.
Aligned with anguish,
arrayed in agony.
Wandering aimlessly through darkness,
searching for that which cannot be found.
Standing at the precipice,
trying to weight it all out.
Coming up empty each time and again.
One enormous step . . .

but something breaks my fall

A sudden silhouette framed in silvery light,
pierces the murky mounds.
With love You look upon me,
offering an outstretched hand.

You speak peace.
The billows cease to roll,
and the clouds break.
You command stillness, on both land and sea
as well as in my tortured soul.

Now Your smile is all my warmth and sunshine,
Your arm a shelter in the time of storm.
Eyes as bright as the north star,
lighting a path, to the blessed shore,
leading this troubled heart home.

3/17/01

Seron Wright Jr.

MONDAY

Resolution

"Enjoy your trip, Mr. Wright," says the airport security guard at the last checkpoint in the O'Hare terminal.

"Thank you," I reply.

That next morning, I woke up feeling a little lighter and more grounded all at the same time. I spot Rodney anxiously awaiting me just on the other side of the threshold. It is as if the sight of Rodney completes a circuit, coming together with the revived feelings of love from my God, my family, my friends, and myself.

"Good morning," I call out as we walk over to each other.

"Mine is a lot better now," he replies. "You enjoy the weekend?"

"You know what, I really did."

He takes my carry-on bag for me.

"That's good. So you ready to go?" he asks.

"Not quite."

A look of worry replaces the smile he was flashing just a moment ago. I reach down and take his hand in mine.

"Now I'm ready," I answer.

His face quickly cycles from concern, passed confusion and settles on contentment.

"Cool," he replies, grinning.

We turn and make our way through the terminal, oblivious of everyone and everything around us on the way to something infinite.

TO MY RESCUE

Held captive, oh so long
imprisoned by fears and heartaches

A slave to Lord solitude,
yoked between contempt and despair

Then came you, my angel
answering unuttered prayers

A shining ebon knight,
charging up on a sable steed

Wielding cords of love,
you scaled my walls

Armed with a silver smile,
you banished my demons

Kneeling down you touched my heart,
making an instant connection

My shackles shatter
in the light of your eyes

Swept up into your arms
Pure poetry in motion

Riding away into sunsets
long ago forgotten

Contemplating happily ever afters,
thought forever elusive

Singing praises from a
heart once frozen

All because of you
coming to my rescue

3/17/01

Seron Wright Jr.

Excerpt for Love: From Behind

Seron and Rodney are on the road to learning how to love each other, but what about Lee? Remember Seron's workplace crush? Sure you do.

It took all of my resolve to get through that interview without getting lost in those dark brown eyes, not to be mesmerized by his gorgeous light bronze face. The last couple of months working so close to his compact swimmer's build within the campus Academic Advising office were the sweetest torture.—Seron

* * *

Lee admits a small pang of envy at Seron and Rodney's "perfect" relationship . . . Seron occasionally inspired a skipped heartbeat or two as well as no small number of erections for Lee.

"I could have had either of them," he smiles to himself. "Hell! Both!"

While Seron moves about the room preparing to go into the shower, Lee sits on his own bed and eyes him intently. Seron is totally pre-occupied. He walks to the night stand between the two beds. Lee swiftly but silently moves to sit facing Seron's bed, rears back and lays a resounding "SLAP" on Seron's nearly naked ass.

Lee presses his body up against him and holds him there as his free hand roughly cups his tight little ass. He moves in for a kiss. After meager resistance, Seron's lips part allowing Lee's tongue to enter. Seron slowly relaxes into Lee's grasp. Lee releases his hands, removes Seron's boxers, and turns him around to face the bed. There Lee places him on the bed face first. For the briefest second Lee admires his handy work before starting to "wax and tenderize" his new ride.

* * *

Now that we've watched one man's journey to finding something infinite, let's flip the coin and look at how another does everything to avoid it in *Love: From Behind* available Fall 2011.

Something Infinite Discussion Questions

Co-authored and edited by Louis Spraggins

1) **Seron's mental journey to the past and his trip to Chicago is largely driven by his unresolved break up with his first love, Calvin.**
    a. Think back to the very first person you ever felt you were romantically in love with.
        i. What was it that caused you and that person to end your relationship?

2) **Seron and Calvin's relationship comes to an end due to the latter not being able to live with the former's HIV+ status.**
    a. All… or at least MOST of us have what some call "deal breakers."
        i. What do you consider to be a deal breaker; what would make you leave or end a relationship with someone you feel you're madly in love with?
    b. Sometimes, feeling that we're in love makes us take risks we wouldn't normally take.
        i. What are some risks you've taken in the name of love that you wouldn't have taken if you weren't in love?

3) **One of the central themes of this work is Seron's conflicting ideas about his sexuality (loving another man) and spirituality (loving God).**
    a. Are there some things you've done in your life that might clash with your spiritual beliefs?
        i. Name a few and tell why you feel they clash with your spiritual beliefs.

4) **Throughout the novel Seron wrestles with not being able to love himself because he rejects being homosexual.**
    a. We all have things about ourselves that we don't necessarily like.

i. Which of your characteristics or behaviors (past or present) do you dislike SO MUCH that you would give or do anything to change them?
ii. Why do you dislike this/these things about yourself so much?

5) **One of the most evident emotions expressed in this work is the love between Seron and his friends.**
    a. Think of your closest friends, those who you feel will be your friends for the rest of your life.
        i. What experiences have you shared with those friends that cemented your friendships and let you just KNOW you will be friends for life?

6) **Seron's continued attempts to hide his relationship to Rodney illustrate that he might not be as ready for a relationship and might not know as much about what it takes to love another as he initially thought.**
    a. As we go through life and experience relationships, we learn and we grow. Think back to your first experiences of romantic love.
        i. Have any of your views of what love is or what love does changed?
        ii. What are the differences between how you saw love then and how you see love now?
        iii. What experience did you have that made you change your view of love?

7) **After some time Seron admits to himself that he ran away from Chicago and his past.**
    a. Sometimes, we may find ourselves in situations or dealing with issues in our life that are SO overwhelming that we feel we just cannot deal with it, so we just walk (or run) away from them.
        i. What situations or issues have you run from?
        ii. What made them so intense that you just had to get away from them?

8) **As Seron moves through the novel he learns and acquires love in various forms.**
   Define or describe love in your own words.

9) **At the end of the novel Seron's mother reminds him of his lifelong dream to become a published author, a dream he lives.**
   What dreams and aspirations have you yet to fulfill?

10) **Seron recalls many close calls due to unsafe sex practices and ironically contracting HIV partially due his attempts to hide his life style.**

    What more do you think can be done to make all people more comfortable discussing sex and safe sex practices.

End Prompt for group: "Close your eyes. Think back to that terrible time, that lonely time. When you were certain that everyone and everything was against you. When you desperately wished for any kind word, gesture, helping hand, expression of love. Think of that odd person, that different person, the person everyone talks bad about. That person you occasionally look down on, laugh at, talk about and think less of. Can you picture them clearly? Good. Now think about any small thing you might do to show them that you see them as a person, that they matter that someone in world loves them just as any stranger, any human being can show compassion to another. Finally, make up in your mind to do it and love infinitely."

"Praise for Love: Something Infinite"

"Seron is on a journey to embracing love, realizing that it is not judgmental or conditional, that one's capacity to give and receive it is endless . . . [He] stands in as an (Black SGL) Everyman. Struggling to define manhood—and, by extension, himself—in a world that too often refuses to recognize him as a man."—James Earl Hardy, Author of the bestselling B-Boy Blues Series.

"A poetic flow of story, dialogue and prose capture literary elegance in author Eddie S. Pierce's body of work, 'Love:Something Infinite.'"—LaToya Cross, N'Digo

"Since the untimely death of writer E. Lynn Harris, there has been a void in the gay African-American literary community. Chicago-based Eddie S. Pierce's debut novel 'Love: Something Infinite' could change all that."—Gregg Shapiro, WisconsinGazette.com

Author Biography:

Eddie S. Pierce is a Master's of Fine Arts in Creative Writing degree recipient from Chicago State University, home of the world renowned Gwendolyn Brooks Writing Center and host of the annual Gwendolyn Brooks Writer's Conference. Mr. Pierce considers himself to be primarily a fiction and prose writer but has recently been afforded the opportunity to be published in 95Notes Literary Magazine for poetry and Sage Publishing's Encyclopedia of Identity for an article on the phenomena of "Passing." On Saturday, November 12, 2011 Pierce released his first self-published work, "Love: Something Infinite" and simultaneously launched Rainbow Room Publishing. Additionally he is currently producing more titles and pursuing numerous other literary ventures. Eddie **is a native of** Chicago, IL.

Made in the USA
Middletown, DE
02 December 2022